"So, what did you call this? My unplanned plan?"

Natalie smiled. "Yep, you have some great ideas, even if the event planner wasn't on board at first. Thanks for this." She nodded down at the centerpiece.

"You're welcome. It's a good reminder for you."

"A reminder?"

"That you're beautiful." He'd said it then, and he meant it now, more than ever. She blushed, but a coughing fit brought Thad to his senses. "You need to go inside. The temp is dropping by the second."

She nodded as she continued to cough into her upper arm, since the centerpiece was in her hands. "Thank you so much, Thad. Pray I get better for the festival." He nodded and she hurried into the house.

Thad spun around, wanting to jump in childish glee. He hadn't been this happy in a long time. And it had little to do with fishing.

Just a couple weeks ago, Thad's plan for a fresh start in Rapid Falls to be close to Brody seemed to be enough. But then Natalie showed up...and offered something he'd forgotten about.

Texas transplant **Angie Dicken** lives in Iowa with her family of six, balancing a busy schedule of school sports and activities, date nights with her husband and get-togethers with her longtime friends. Setting sweet romance stories in the beloved heartland seems as natural as sweet corn in the summer and snowplows in the thick of winter. Angie is a multi-published author and an ACFW member. Check out her books and news of upcoming releases at www.angiedicken.com.

Visit the Author Profile page at LoveInspired.com.

The Unplanned Christmas Family

ANGIE DICKEN

LOVE INSPIRED
INSPIRATIONAL ROMANCE

LOVE INSPIRED®
INSPIRATIONAL ROMANCE

Recycling programs
for this product may
not exist in your area.

ISBN-13: 978-1-335-93687-5

The Unplanned Christmas Family

Copyright © 2024 by Angie Dicken

Love Inspired
22 Adelaide St. West, 41st Floor
Toronto, Ontario M5H 4E3, Canada
www.LoveInspired.com

Printed in Lithuania

MIX
Paper | Supporting
responsible forestry
FSC® C021394

Glory to God in the highest,
and on earth peace, good will toward men.
—*Luke* 2:14

To Ashley. Thank you for being there for all my ups and downs, for speaking truth to me always and for believing in me when I need it most! Love you!

Chapter One

Natalie slammed on the brakes, a reckless reaction to her tires slipping on the slick, snowy patch. What was she thinking? She'd driven on Iowa roads since she was fourteen years old—her debut behind the wheel with Dad gently guiding her through the Jim's Grocery parking lot. Now, she was clutching the steering wheel tightly and frantically pumping her brakes to correct her initial pedal to the floor. Her sedan ground to a halt, just before hitting the retirement center's yard sign for their annual Christmas Festival—exactly one month away. Yikes. Natalie rolled her eyes. Even in a near accident she was paying attention to details.

"Natalie, are you there?" Her best friend, Lindsey, spoke through her car speakers.

"Barely." She swiped loose curls away from her eyes and turned up the speaker volume. "Sorry, didn't hear what you said, Lindsey."

"It's no biggie. Is everything okay?"

Natalie pressed her back in the seat and tried to catch her breath. "Be glad I am speaking right now. You may have been having a conversation with sirens had my sanity not kicked in last minute."

"What? What happened? I was worried about you heading home in this mess." A flurry of children's voices sounded in the background. "I-20 is an ice rink."

"I just pulled into my grandmother's retirement community. We're having Thanksgiving dinner with her and fifty of her closest friends." Natalie smiled. She couldn't wait to hug Gigi and the knitting club ladies. "I, uh, I need to get out of this car…and get rid of the boxes from the Matthews wedding. They are taunting me from the back seat, distracting me with regrets from our last event of the year."

Lindsey gasped. "The wedding was a huge success! You are far too hard on yourself, Natalie. Exactly why you need a break. A good ole-fashioned Christmas break."

"I never thought I would pass up a trip to Arizona with my parents during an Iowa winter. But honestly, the fact that I was so lost in thought about how I could've made our last event even better that my winter driving skills escaped me, I am pretty sure cozying up at home for a few weeks is absolutely necessary." Natalie craved the downtime alone. Being a sought-after event planner and having just spent a month in Texas with a very high-maintenance bride, a wintry stay at home was the very best Christmas plan right now. Even if her parents were leaving for sunny Scottsdale tomorrow, Natalie didn't mind pet-sitting her favorite golden retriever, Lex, and joining Gigi for a weekly cribbage game or two.

"I just called to say Happy Thanksgiving." Lindsey then whispered something to someone who sounded about knee-high.

"Happy Thanksgiving. Let me know if anything comes up."

"Nope, won't do that." Lindsey snickered. "We agreed, no shop talk till January. Right?"

"Right." Natalie moved her rearview mirror to get those leftover boxes of wedding favors out of her view. She meant to drop them off at her storage unit but was anxious to get home when she got to town. "No more planning anything but cocoa, a fire and scheduled naptime."

"Sounds divine. If my nephews continue to require my undivided attention, I might sneak away and join you."

"My apartment is open for the taking." Natalie smiled to herself. Her staycation officially started this morning when she moved her toiletries to her parents' guest bathroom—about twenty yards from her garage apartment on the other side of their driveway. She'd hardly been home this past fall—staying at extended-stay hotels while fully investing in three brides, a corporate awards banquet and the most amazing Cystic Fibrosis Gala, raising money for the foundation to continue its lifesaving work. Natalie should be completely satisfied. Their little event planning company had plenty of financial cushion for a restful winter. But that tweak in her chest reminded her that taking a break didn't happen quite so easily. She must rest, though. Her new high blood pressure diagnosis was a wake-up call, especially since her late grandfather suffered from a heart attack brought on by years of a high stress career.

After saying goodbye to Lindsey, Natalie took some calming breaths just like her therapist had advised. But on the fifth breath, a knock on her window startled the calm right back out of her.

"Excuse me?"

All Natalie could make out on the other side of the frosty glass was a winter coat with a plaid scarf tucked beneath faux fur lining.

The person knocked again. "Hey, you're in an accessible space."

Natalie rolled her window down and looked up. A guy around her age with a five-o'clock shadow, narrowing eyes and a plastered-on smile that may have undertones of passive-aggressiveness stared down out her.

"Sorry, I kinda slid in here. That sign was a near-casualty." Natalie nervously giggled—more like a bride with cold feet than the even-keeled event planner she had become.

"Glad you're safe," he said, sounding as though he felt obligated to, before continuing, "But do you mind moving soon? We are expecting a full house."

The familiar *I-have-a-whole-event-on-my-shoulders* tone seemed to set the guy's jaw to working.

"Of course. If you don't mind stepping back, I can't guarantee that my slippy wheels won't roll right over your—" She looked down. He was wearing snow boots along with coveralls. Must be the maintenance guy. She should tell him to consider salting the parking lot a little more. Slipping and sliding was hardly a Thanksgiving welcome. Instead, Natalie rolled up her window, carefully backed out and found a space near her parents' truck. She grabbed her purse and crammed her knit hat over her curly brown hair. Using the rearview mirror to check her lip gloss, she spied those pesky boxes in her back seat again, and forced herself to look away.

"Well, at least I stopped thinking about work for a hot minute, even if it was because of cute Mr. Grumpy Pants." She blushed at her terminology. She was *not* a teen describing a boy across the classroom. Just because that maintenance guy definitely was handsome didn't mean her hot minute had anything to do with him. It had everything to do with getting lost in thoughts about event planning and not paying attention to her driving.

Besides, the male prospects in Rapid Falls were the last thing Natalie wanted to think about. Her life was busy enough—exactly why she hadn't dated much. After she had worked so hard to get where she was, most relationships fizzled with her inattention to the guy and her devotion to her next event. And when it hadn't, she'd almost risked everything. She couldn't exchange this dream she was living for only a potential fairy-tale life of romance. Natalie stepped onto a cleared patch of pavement and carefully walked down the sidewalk to the front doors of Rapid Falls Retirement Center, breathing in the scent of exhaust, clean winter air and—cologne?

She turned around. The maintenance guy was right behind her.

"Let me get that for you." He whisked by and held open the door. "Happy Thanksgiving." Ah, now the parking police had become the welcome committee.

"Happy Thanksgiving to you." He offered a genuine smile now. Natalie cleared her throat and said, "You might want to salt that particular area of the parking lot, though. It's slippery."

His smile remained on his lips but fell away from his eyes. "Once you head inside, that's my plan." And he shifted his weight and opened and closed his gloved fingers around the door handle. If Natalie lingered any longer, she imagined his waterproof boots would start tapping against the brick porch.

She weakly smiled and stepped into the warm lobby. The guy faded into the wintry background, while the ambers, golds and browns of harvest decor wrapped her in an inviting hug. The bustling dining room entrance was framed with raffia garland and orange-and-white-checkered bows. Her parents were taking their seats with Gigi at a round table closest to the entrance. They had left a few minutes before Natalie while she finished unpacking from her recent trip down south.

Natalie shook off her coat as she approached them. "Happy Thanksgiving!"

Gigi tilted her head and smiled. "My girl is home for a

while. So very glad." She rose from her seat and held open her arms. Natalie embraced the woman who smelled of the familiar expensive perfume—Gigi's signature scent that hinted to her personality—rich and flowery but heart-deep warmth.

"I am so glad to be home." Natalie sighed as she sat between Mom and Gigi, and they both took turns giving her a hug.

Gigi primped silver hair that framed her heart-shaped face. "Oh, here come the gals."

In one bubbling gaggle, Gigi's knitting club ladies moved across the dining room and filled in the rest of the seats around the table. Exclamatory greetings popcorned from each, but Susie Fredrickson bypassed her own seat and came over and squeezed Natalie.

"It's so good to see you again." Susie's voice was soft and squishy, like her hug. "Girls, you should have seen the Cystic Fibrosis Gala this lady planned."

"Susie has raved about your event, Natalie." Gigi patted her friend's arm. "Exactly why we know Natty will do great things around here, too."

Natalie gave Gigi a second glance. What did she mean? If winning a few cribbage games and making a mean cup of hot chocolate, then sure, she'd do great things around here. She took off her hat and primped her own hair.

Susie continued to speak as she crossed over to her seat. "It was an absolute dream night—especially for those CF superheroes. I still can't get over the stories—that Tate Behrens from Polk Center just stuck with me. He's not letting CF keep him from living life to the fullest."

One of the other ladies from the knitting club teased, "I think that boy is a local celebrity in Rapid Falls after the umpteenth time Susie's told his story." Everyone laughed.

Susie remarked, "One day, I won't just be on the retirement community board, but I'll make this place home, too, and you'll get to hear my stories at breakfast, lunch and dinner. Just you wait." She winked at Natalie. Susie was a longtime schoolteacher and had been a dear mentor to Natalie over the years. At first, with dyslexia tutoring at the end of middle school, and then, inspiring Natalie to reach for the stars through high school. If it wasn't for Susie… Natalie shuddered to consider how she may have never had the courage to start her own business with Lindsey. Not with her learning disability wreaking havoc on her self-esteem during those earlier years.

While everyone filled Natalie in on the news around Rapid Falls, she tried to focus on the cheery conversation. She was home, and she didn't have one client vying for her attention. All events had been wrapped in a neat bow of accomplishment, even if she had a tendency of recalling imperfections after the fact. Also, that small, annoying voice in the back of Natalie's mind distracted her too much. *What if you lose too much steam?*

The battle was real. She'd given so much of herself to her work, she wasn't sure who she was without it. Maybe Lindsey *should* move here to keep her in vacation mode.

Feedback from a microphone caused everyone to wince, and conversations around the room quieted. A familiar man in a suit and tie stood at the mic by the buffet table decked out with several cornucopias among platters of food.

"Happy Thanksgiving, everyone." The man's genuine greeting caused a ripple of happy responses in return. Natalie realized he was the parking attendant. No coveralls and boots, but slimming gray slacks and a fitted sweater over a collared shirt. A charming transformation. Natalie leaned over to question who this parking-lot-attendant-turned-speaker was, when instead of Gigi, the guy said, "I am Thad MacDougall, the center's director. I've only been here for a few months, but the kindness and welcome I've received in Rapid Falls has quickly made this town feel like home. I personally have so much to be thankful for." He offered that dashing smile that Natalie previewed at the door—before her unsolicited advice killed the moment. "I'd like to say grace over this amazing spread."

Everyone bowed their heads. Thad said an eloquent prayer filled with gratitude and faith. Amens filled the room, then tables were released to the buffet.

While their table waited, the knitting club's most vocal member, Tina Delaney, leaned forward, crushing her festive place setting with her faux suede vest. "Quite a catch, huh?" Her piercing eyes danced with matchmaking mischief.

Natalie slid a glance at Mom and Dad. They both gave her an apologetic look, as was often their response when Gigi's friends tried to suggest the perfect guy for Natalie. Even if Rapid Falls was a small town, it seemed that single men found their way here on occasion. Over the years, there had only been a handful of attempts, but still, Natalie figured out the perfect response: "My dance card is full. The last date has promise."

And even if it had been several months since her last date, the ladies didn't need to know. They usually backed off a bit, satisfied that at least Natalie was doing the good work of making a match herself. Honestly, her heart wasn't in it at this point in her life. The last guy had proved to be a threat to all she held dear as an entrepreneur. But, of course, she'd never explain that to these lovely ladies.

Tina's eyes flashed, her gaze shifted above Natalie's head and, for the first time, she refuted Natalie's excuse. "You're not married yet. Option debonair heading your way."

Natalie looked over her shoulder. Thad MacDougall walked up, placing a hand on Gigi's shoulder and greeting the ladies, who were leaning much closer to the table's center than before. Gone was Gigi's pretty perfume. Now all Natalie could smell was cedar and mint and handsome. When Thad looked at her, he hesitated before saying, "You're Fran's granddaughter?"

Natalie nodded and smiled. *And you are just a pawn in the knitting club's favorite yarnless pastime. Back away, Thad, just back away.*

Thad wasn't one to pass judgment on strangers. After all, he had struggled with being misjudged the last couple of years by his ex-wife. But as Tina, Susie and Fran doted on Natalie, he returned a tight smile. All he could think about was the many emails that this supposed renowned event planner in the greater part of the Midwest had ignored.

Not one response as he managed the Christmas Festival planning committee—a task he had no desire taking on these first few months of adjusting to a new town, job and shared custody of his nine-year-old son, Brody. But if there was one thing he could say about Rapid Falls—and especially its beloved retirement center—is that they loved their community events, and the Christmas Festival was an unspoken responsibility of the retirement community director.

Fran clapped her hands and said to Natalie, "Now you two have met face-to-face, isn't that nice?"

Natalie gave a confused smile and nod. Did she not realize who he was? He had introduced himself in at least one of the emails, and followed up with a reminder of who he was in the next couple.

A dinner volunteer dismissed the table to the buffet line.

Fran held out a hand for help, and as Thad moved to assist, Natalie's hand grabbed his accidentally. She flicked her curly auburn hair from her shoulder as she popped up from her chair, dropped her hand and exclaimed, "I was going to help my grandmother. Promise." A deep dimple appeared in her rosy cheek and her blue eyes sparkled with apology.

Thad stepped back, ignoring the warmth of her slender fingers wrapping around his palm. "Of course," he confirmed. "And I was going to help her, too. She's one of the lovely ladies who've made this a smooth transition for me."

"Isn't he such a gentleman." Fran gleamed up at Thad while speaking to her granddaughter.

"And a jack-of-all-trades, I take it." Natalie tucked her grandmother's arm in hers as they scooted past. "Parking lot attendant, greeter and director—"

"Don't forget, Christmas Festival manager." Thad shoved his hands in his pockets, glancing around at the bustling room shrouded by a harvest decor explosion. But he didn't miss the opportunity to examine Natalie's reaction to his words.

She didn't flinch at the mention. "You have a lot on your plate, it sounds like." Natalie sighed in empathy. Fran was distracted by conversation with the other ladies, not appearing miffed at all that her granddaughter wasn't helping with the supposed festival plans, either.

Heat crept around Thad's starched collar—had Natalie even told Fran that she wasn't going to be part of this year's festival? If he recalled correctly, a month ago, Fran had been over the moon the day she gave him Natalie's email. What was it she said before slipping him a folded paper with a handwritten email address?

"Natalie is one of few young people who treasure this place as much as the residents. Finally slowing down for the holidays, she's all in to help."

All in.

Hmph. Before Thad could breathe in a better attitude along with the buttery aroma of fresh rolls mixed with rosemary, thyme and all the goodness of a Thanksgiving spread, his phone vibrated in his pocket. He stepped away from the dining room and answered.

"Hey, bud. Happy Thanksgiving."

"I have a stomachache," Brody mumbled.

"Too much pie?"

"I don't know. Maybe I should just stay here."

Thad clenched his teeth and ignored the heaviness in his heart. He cleared his throat and forced a playful tone. "What? And miss out on watching football together?"

"I can just watch it here." Brody's tendency to try and back out of plans was exactly why Thad moved close by.

"I'll tell you what, just come over and if you don't feel good, I can take care of you. I have a whole liter of ginger ale with your name on it."

A long pause followed. Finally, Brody said, "Okay."

"See you at seven. Mom's bringing you to the center, right?"

"Mom, are you bringing me to the center?" Thad could hear Maxine affirm in the background.

"Great. Love you, bud."

Thad ended the call. He wanted his son to depend on him in all aspects of his life—not just the occasional fun outing. And especially when he didn't feel well. A child should want their parent at that time. However, during the two years of working on his MBA and job hunting after, Thad hadn't been that type of caregiver. How could he have been? He had worked late, then studied even later. Life had been chaos back then. Brody was barely talking when Thad started his master's program, and by the time Thad had landed his first job after, kindergarten for his son was over—a bittersweet season of professional accomplishment with a marriage dissolved by his wife's emotional attachment to another guy who had been there for her during Thad's program. He couldn't blame her. And he really couldn't expect Brody to latch on to him now that Thad had moved to a new town.

But even his ex, Maxine, looked forward to having Thad nearby while she and her new husband traveled quite a bit. Thad's gut twisted when Brody didn't seem easily attached to Thad—the father who was distant mentally for a couple of years, and then living two hours away that first year after the divorce.

"Everything okay, Thad?" The spritely Susie Fredrickson, volunteer activity coordinator, stood at the dining room entrance holding her plate of turkey, stuffing, corn casserole and green beans. "You look...conflicted."

"Brody is trying to back out of our plans together." He sighed. Susie had been his first acquaintance in Rapid Falls. She was a board member and on the hiring team when Thad interviewed and showed him around town when he first arrived. She had a way with kids, and although Brody appeared shy when Thad first brought him to the retirement community's center, Susie had his son refusing to leave until they finished a mean game of Go Fish.

Susie tilted her head and raised her brows above fashionable glasses. "Holidays are especially hard on kids when change is involved. Don't worry. Just keep being your amazing self." She winked. He smiled and followed her into the dining room again.

"Hey, Susie?"

She set her plate down and looked over at him.

The brief conversation with Brody awakened his usual unease about his commitment to work. Another reason he was annoyed with Natalie's unresponsiveness. He wasn't going to spend his time planning an event if it took time away from mending his relationship with his son, especially during Christmas. He drew closer to the table between them and said, "Has Fran mentioned anything about Nat—"

"What's that, dear?" Fran walked up behind him. He pulled her chair out for her and tried to reframe his inquiry since Natalie returned to her seat, as well.

Thad stepped back and shoved his hands in his pockets. While everyone filled in the table, he crouched down for a conversation with just the two women, steadying himself with a hand on Fran's chair back. "I just wanted to chat about the Christmas Festival."

Fran gave him her full attention, but Natalie was digging into her mashed potatoes. Thad's stomach growled as Fran replied, "Oh, yes. It's quite a feat, but I trust that it will be a success with the two of you in the same town now."

Natalie continued eating.

Thad wasn't sure what was going on. Was her granddaughter so famished that she didn't want to converse right now?

"With an event like this, it's ideal for planning to start a couple months out, at least," Thad grumbled. "Especially now that the save-the-dates have been mailed."

"Ah, yes. Have you all made lot of headway?" Fran craned her head to catch her granddaughter's eye.

"What's that?" Natalie wiped her mouth with her napkin.

"Thad was just talking about plans for the Christmas Festival." Fran smiled wide. "Natalie's been to so many, you all are no doubt close to having it all planned out."

Natalie furrowed her brow, tossing a confused look between Fran and Thad. "Who? Me? I haven't thought about the Christmas Festival until I nearly ran into the sign out in the parking lot." Her laugh faded quickly as she seemed to notice the somber look that Thad managed instead of a scowl. "Um, it's December twenty-third, right?"

Fran chuckled and swatted at Natalie's arm. "Oh, dear,

you are a hoot. You younger kids have 'just kidding' down to an art."

"Gigi, what are you talking about?"

"You're helping with the planning, dear. Don't be silly."

Natalie's eyes rounded, she turned toward her mother on the other side of her—as if seeking clarification, but her mom wasn't paying attention—and then back at Fran, this time pulling her legs from under the table to face Fran straight on.

"I never agreed to plan anything, Gigi," Natalie near-whispered.

"You could have replied to one of my emails and clued me in." Thad shouldn't have allowed that snark to slip out. But he'd felt pretty slighted this past month, and with all the pressure for work-life balance, his nerves were about to snap like a wishbone.

"Emails?" Natalie seemed completely unaware—as if he was speaking a different language.

Thad exhaled an "Oh, boy," and stood up. "So, you never received my emails about planning the dinner and pageant?"

Fran shook her head and gave an audible guffaw. "Now, Natalie, when you called for my birthday back in October, we squared it all away. You'd be home for a while, and I said the festival needed your expertise. You agreed."

"And I'd sent you about four emails since then," Thad added. "You are a supposed planning guru, and by your permission, according to Fran, I assigned you as head co-ordinator."

Natalie crossed her legs, her brown boot kicking at the white tablecloth. She pressed a finger to her temple and closed her eyes tight, her lips tighter. "Gigi, I agreed that I would be happy to help with the festival, *while I am in town*." Her eyes popped open and pure shock hardened every feature. "But to *plan* it?" Her voice went up an octave or two. "I am sorry, I just can't."

Discomfort from this awkward confrontation wrapped around Thad's shoulders as tight as his hunger pangs from smelling, seeing but not tasting the Thanksgiving feast. The two women seemed utterly confused with hurt crossing each of their faces. But he still wasn't sure how Natalie could have been so oblivious when he had communicated succinctly. "Do you not check your email?" he blurted.

Natalie turned to him and quirked an eyebrow. "Excuse me? I am a professional. Of course I check my email."

"And you get the weekly newsletter from the retirement center, right? I saw your name on the subscriber list."

Natalie nodded. "And did you use my email from that list?"

Thad began to nod, but then froze. "Well, I guess I used the email Fran wrote down. I wasn't at my computer so…" He pulled out his phone and opened his email app. "Your email is Natalie underscore Cooper at—"

"Dash," Natalie said.

"What?"

"Natalie dash Cooper." Her brow rose in apology. "You got the wrong email address. I had no idea you were trying to reach me. Hopefully you've moved ahead without me."

Thad hadn't really. He'd gotten some local businesses to commit to the silent auction, had his secretary mail out updated save-the-dates using last year's document, and he'd set up a meeting with a local caterer. But that was it.

Thad MacDougall was by no means a planner. He was a single father with the weight of his son's distance on his heart and a slightly soured appetite for Thanksgiving dinner. He seemed to be responsible for the success of the retirement community's favorite festival all on his own.

Chapter Two

Natalie was perplexed how the director of a thriving business and beloved home to so many residents could make the rookie mistake of not double-checking an email when he hadn't received a response. Of course, Natalie would have nipped the idea of taking on the event at the very root of such a suggestion. But still. The Christmas Festival was quite an undertaking—why wouldn't he persist on seeking input?

Maybe he didn't really need help, but obliged Gigi by reaching out? His worry lines and obvious annoyance over unread emails said otherwise.

The usual pressure sat on Natalie's chest at the thought of not only helping but having been absent from a whole month of planning. If there was one thing Natalie Cooper couldn't stand, it was being late to the game. Exactly why her business thrived. She could not rest in the shadows of others and miss out on her own ideas and decisions being considered. She'd spent several years feeling like she was in an eternal game of playing catch-up, and finally, this past season of success proved that she had arrived at a very cushy earned seat at the proverbial table of event planners and small business owners. And while her effort came with the reward of jobs well done, she'd also paid the price in a physical toll.

When Thad walked away with a quick, "No worries. We'll figure it out," Natalie absorbed Gigi's worried stare.

"Certainly you can help, dear?"

Knowing she'd been misunderstood during a time when Natalie was her busiest wasn't nearly as upsetting as the fact that Gigi had counted on her for help she just couldn't give. Natalie could either tell her about her blood pressure or ignore her disappointment as best as she could. She chose the latter so as to not worry her grandmother.

Natalie plastered a smile on her face. "Sounds like Thad has it covered, Gigi. But I will be around here for any advice." Gigi's helping of sweet potato casserole gave her a chance to change the subject. "Those are perfectly roasted marshmallows, don't you think?"

Gigi visibly sighed and looked at her plate. "Your favorite, dear."

"Yes, ma'am." Natalie giggled away the last of her anxiety, assured that she'd just escaped the temptation to go against her doctor's orders, and Lindsey's. She re-embraced the most important thing this moment—the delicious array of savory and sweet delectables on her plate and the familiar faces who radiated affection.

Her gaze snagged on Thad MacDougall, finishing up in the buffet line.

Mom leaned toward her from her right. "Thad has done wonders around here."

Natalie dropped her attention to her food. "Oh, I think I recall Gigi raving about the dashing director, come to think about it." During the same phone call when she had misunderstood the amount of help Gigi had been asking Natalie to give.

Mom took a bite of turkey and cranberry sauce. *Her* favorite. "Thad's got a little boy who adores Lex. Brody comes here after school with Thad, sometimes. And the man is such a caring father. He actually moved to Rapid Falls to be close to his son."

"Oh?" Natalie noticed Thad taking a seat next to the nurse practitioner, Edward Shaw, and elderly Hal Kerr. "Do I know the boy's mother?" Rapid Falls was a small town, after all. Not many people moved here as adults, unless they were returning to their childhood hometown to raise a family.

"No. I believe she—Maxine—and her husband, Derek, bought a home with acreage north of town a year ago." Mom sighed. "According to Thad, and all the ladies who love to talk—" Mom grinned, her blue eyes flashing as she partook in gabbing like knitting club fashion "—Thad couldn't stand only seeing Brody on the weekends. So, when the director position opened up, he jumped at it." She smiled. "It's refreshing to see Thad and Maxine's cordial relationship with each other. They work together to do what's best for their son, even if they aren't married anymore."

Natalie smiled. She glanced at her dad on the other side of Mom. He was conversing with a knitting club lady's husband. Natalie was ever thankful to have two parents who also did what was best for her, all her life.

A server interrupted, offering decaf. Mom happily raised her coffee cup and delightfully cooed, "Thank you," when her cup was full. Mom dazzled everyone with her elegance and piercing blue eyes that captured whomever she was talking to in an assurance that her attention was fully theirs. Natalie forgot how much she loved spending time with her mother. If only she and Dad weren't heading to Arizona first thing in the morning.

While Natalie finished her food, Mom leaned back, holding her steaming cup in her hands in pure relaxation mode. "You know, Lex loves coming to the center. She enjoys the attention, and the residents have crowned her their favorite golden retriever."

"That's nice. I'd love to bring her here." Natalie turned to Gigi again to ask about their postponed cribbage game from the last time Natalie had visited. But Gigi was in deep conversation with Susie. Her frown lines were intense, and Natalie heard her say "Festival" more than once. Natalie opened her mouth to speak, but then decided this really was none of her business.

Like Lindsey would always say, "Not everything is for you to do, Natalie."

But when they finished the meal and gathered in the lobby to say goodbye, Gigi snatched Natalie by the arm and leveled a gaze that any younger version of herself would have paid fearful attention to.

"I need you to promise you will follow up with Thad on this festival business. He seems more than overwhelmed to most of us. As far as Susie can tell, he's got some plans in place, but he's a little nonchalant about the whole thing." She looked over her shoulder like a conspiratress, not the sweet matriarch who made the best no-bake cookies this side of the Mississippi. "If you ask me, he lacks vision." She quirked an eyebrow. "And you know how that goes. Didn't you say your last bride struggled with that?"

Natalie swallowed a laugh. How did this woman take Natalie's observation about her last client tending toward lackadaisical as the same as not having vision? Agreeing to help with the festival's final touches meant, to Gigi, that Natalie signed up as event planner extraordinaire. "Vision is subjective, I think." She winked.

Gigi shrugged her shoulders, looked over at Thad, who was standing like a magazine model with one hand in his pocket and the other one splayed on his torso as he talked with some guests. Quite the vision himself. A trap for Natalie, who knew that beauty was only skin deep in many cases. Her one and only serious boyfriend, handsome as can be, cared more about himself than any of Natalie's ambitions…once they moved past the initial boy-meets-girl phase. A relationship that dragged on far too long, causing setbacks for Natalie's self-esteem back when she was trying to start her business.

"I am so glad you are here, dear." Gigi transformed from skeptical resident to her usual sweet self. She placed a hand on Natalie's cheek. "I shall love winning that game of cribbage you owe me."

Now, Natalie did laugh. "Keep telling yourself that, Gigi." She dipped down and kissed her cheek.

After Mom and Dad hugged Gigi one last time before their trip, Gigi reached for Natalie's arm and whispered in her ear, "Bring Lex with you next time. She'll entertain the boy while you check on the festival plans." She returned a kiss on Natalie's cheek.

The usual pressure threatened as the word *festival* began to take on a whole different meaning to Natalie—once a fun, longtime community event, now a hindrance to her staycation. If only she could shut off that part of her brain that started to imagine the centerpieces and Christmas trees transforming the retirement community into the perfect setting for a dinner and silent auction.

They said their final goodbyes, then Dad offered his wife and daughter an elbow each, like any gentlemanly escort would. He said, "Don't let your grandmother rope you into things around here." Dad's rich voice was like a warm blanket atop Natalie's rising anxiety.

"You noticed?" Natalie half laughed.

"It's all we hear about when we visit her—Thad's direction for the festival is just about to give Gigi a reason to come out of retirement and make Irene proud."

They all laughed. While Gigi hadn't been in the event planning business, she had been a secretary for the family construction business. Supposedly, nothing slipped through the cracks when Gigi had been in charge. Natalie liked to think she'd inherited Gigi's eye for detail.

"It's sweet that she wants to make her sister proud. Aunt Irene founded the festival, after all." They stopped at their cars, Natalie lost in memories of her grandmother's late sister. The iridescent glow of the parking lot lights cast her parents' shadows long against the salted pavement. "Are you sure I am not disappointing her? After all, it's the first festival without Irene here." Her parents bobbed their heads in reverence. Spunky and bright until her last breath. She was sorely missed. "Besides that, if anyone understands Gigi's concern, it's me. Missed details can lead to a disaster." She clenched her teeth as she thought about the inventory in her back seat.

Mom stepped closer and cupped her hand on Natalie's shoulder. "I don't think anyone would let a disaster occur around here. Do not worry one more bit. Your only concern is Lex and bringing some Christmas cheer to Gigi… especially on Christmas Day when we won't be here." Mom glanced up at Dad, exchanging deflated looks. "Are you sure we should leave for so long?"

Natalie now became the voice of reason. "Mother, if anyone needs this, it's you and Dad. You both finally have a chance to spend time with your best friend during the most wonderful time of year."

Mom's eyes brightened. "I do miss spending time with her."

"So, while I take care of Gigi, you enjoy Celia. Before you know it, we'll be spending New Year's Day around your kitchen table nibbling on monkey bread." Natalie hugged her mom and smiled brightly at Dad, who winked with affirmation. She pulled away. "I've got Lex, Gigi and a keen eye for last-minute details on the festival—" Dad opened his mouth to speak but Natalie clarified "—*if* it is needed. In the meantime, maybe I will distract Gigi from all her worrying with the best Cooper tradition of Thanksgiving weekend—" She rubbed her hands together. "Choosing our Christmas tree. Please tell me Rapid Falls Christmas Tree farm is still up and running."

Her parents laughed. Dad nodded exuberantly. "It sure is. And I think you've got a great idea—get Gigi away from the retirement center a bit and focus on Christmas in all its traditions."

"Outside of the festival," Mom added with her finger punctuating the air. "See you at home."

Natalie got in her car and followed her parents out of the parking lot, cranking up Christmas music from her radio and trying to sing along. But Gigi's worry kept inching into her mind.

Was Natalie being selfish by keeping away from festival planning?

She'd never turned down an event before—and this was one she'd grown up with as a child. She shook her head. Never turning down an event was exactly why she needed this time of rest. Natalie should just tell Gigi, and her parents, that she'd been struggling with hypertension due to stress. This staycation was pretty much prescribed.

Probably not the best idea to say something... That would heap unnecessary worry on her parents as they traveled across the country. And Gigi and her friends would treat her like a fragile porcelain doll.

If there was another thing Natalie enjoyed about being home in Rapid Falls—besides the fact it truly was her favorite place in the world—it was that she wasn't seen as fragile anymore—she was a successful business owner.

Her weaker days of being the one in remedial classes, in tutoring and basically unable to keep up with her class-mates were far in the past.

Natalie would not share her latest threat to this claim to local fame as a strong, independent professional—her pesky health issue—because she'd promised Lindsey, her doctor and herself that she was strong enough to resist any undue stress this Christmas. Immersing in family tradi-tions like choosing a Christmas tree was the perfect solu-tion to warding off chest pangs, while also keeping Gigi happily entertained.

So she hoped.

Thad excused himself from the group of residents gath-ered around the main living area fireplace when he saw Maxine and Brody enter the lobby. Brody had a white-knuckled grip on his backpack straps, and his straight blond hair was neatly swept across his forehead—evidence of a mother's touch. His big brown eyes weren't happy or sad, and he nibbled on his lip until he saw Thad, then the cor-ners of his mouth twitched. Did his eyes just shine a little brighter?

Oh, how Thad hoped so. "Hey there. Happy Thanksgiv-ing to you two." He shifted his gaze to his ex-wife.

"Happy Thanksgiving to you." She dipped her chin in a civil way. Just slightly warmer than greeting an acquain-tance. But that was okay. Ever since Thad moved back, he had tried not only to strengthen his relationship with his son but also return to some sort of friendship with Maxine. They were good at being friends before. Now that she was married to a guy that Thad could not begrudge one bit—actually, Derek was someone he could be friends with, too—Maxine seemed less resentful toward Thad, and thankfully, more willing to work out this joint custody with little hesitation.

Brody tugged at Maxine's elbow. She squatted down as he whispered something in her ear. Maxine said, "Sunday night. Not too long." She smiled.

No hesitation on her part, anyway…but obviously from Brody.

"Sunday night will come before you know it, Brody." Thad inwardly winced at his acknowledgment of Brody's wish to just get back to Mom as quickly as possible. Thad looked at his watch, trying to calm his clenching jaw. "Hey, we have about fifteen minutes until kickoff."

Maxine bent down and kissed the top of Brody's head, then gently pushed him toward his father. Thad closed the space between them and took Brody's hand.

"You boys have fun." Maxine smiled, a tweak of concern on her brow as she caught her son's eye. "Don't stay up too late."

"If we do, it will be because of overtime, right, bud?"

Brody nodded. "I'll hope for overtime." A smile finally broke across his round cheeks, activating the dimples that stole the show in all of his baby photos. Thad chuckled, and Maxine rolled her eyes playfully. Besides avoiding bedtime, Brody loved football just like Thad. At least he wasn't being coerced to endure four quarters and a weekend with Dad. The nine-year-old boy was happy company with the game on.

After Thad grabbed his coat from his office and locked up, they headed to his car. "I remote-started so it shouldn't be too cold." When Brody opened the back door, he caught a piece of paper that fluttered to the ground.

"Here, Dad." He handed it to Thad between the driver and passenger seats and then shut the door.

"Ah, do you want to go to that?"

Brody stared at the bright red flyer. Under his breath

he carefully sounded out, "Ch-rist-m…uh, tree farm." He glanced up. "A farm for trees?"

Thad laughed. "A farm for Christmas trees. I thought it might be fun to go pick out a tree and cut it down ourselves this year."

"Really? Like in the movies?" Brody's eyes lit up. "Can I use an ax?"

"I think they use saws. I take it that you want to go there on Saturday?"

"Saturday? Yeah!" Brody stared at the flyer with anticipation.

"Good," Thad exclaimed. "That's the plan." He cranked up the radio to the pregame, and turned onto Birch Lane, the feeder street of the quaint Rapid Falls neighborhood. As he passed by the larger homes, including the historic Victorian with the yard sign touting its recent award as "Remodeled Home of the Year," he said a small prayer in his heart, thankful that he'd earned a parenting point with his son. As they pulled into his driveway, he glanced in the rearview mirror. Brody was staring outside, his turned-up nose close enough to the glass that it was creating a cloudy smudge.

"Dad?" Only his lips moved.

"Yes, son?"

"We should probably be careful of squirrels. Wouldn't want to bring one home with us, right?"

"Right." Thad smiled, his chest welling with warmth at the glimpse of the little guy's thinking wheels turning. "Don't worry. We'll make sure everything is perfect." Brody's anxiety was ever engaged, Thad considered after he pulled into the garage and waited for Brody to follow him in the house. Thad couldn't help but wonder if those years he was minimally present caused any added stress on his child. Back then, Maxine would indicate it had— but Thad couldn't question the past. There was nothing to be done for his lack of focus on his duties as a family man. Or at least, distraction with his studies.

He only had the present moment. And it seemed to be getting better after the initial greeting in the retirement center lobby.

"You put your bag in your room, and I'll get the popcorn."

Brody ran across the hardwood floor to his bedroom. "Don't forget the ginger ale," he called out.

"I won't." Thad headed straight to the fridge to grab the two-liter bottle. His phone began to ring.

"Hello?"

"Thaddeus? This is Fran Cooper." The resident's voice was hushed, as if she were about to divulge a secret. Her granddaughter came to mind and Natalie's doe-eyed look of complete cluelessness at being involved in the festival. Now, the knowledge of the email mishap dissolved his initial irritation with the woman. He couldn't fault her, even if she might need a refresher course on parking etiquette.

"What can I do for you, Miss Fran?" He set the ginger ale on the counter and turned on the television.

Fran cleared her throat. "Well, dear, the Thanksgiving dinner was lovely."

"It was. We have Marge and Lula to thank for coming early and donating their decorating skills."

"Indeed we do. And their desserts were amazing as usual." Fran's laugh warbled a pitch higher than her usual hearty laughter. "But now, dear, we are on the cusp of Christmas. It is quite a shame about your—uh—the misspelled email address."

Brody raced into the room and climbed onto a bar stool, eyeing the waiting two-liter. "Uh, yes, it is. But I have to go—"

"Let me give you Natalie's phone number. She is not

only an expert, but an eyewitness to many past festivals. It would be a shame for her wisdom to go untapped. And, she truly is a delightful creature, if I do say so myself. You will be privileged to get to know her."

Thad sighed and grabbed a notepad on the end table. "Okay, Fran. I'll jot it down." Thad had been frustrated with not receiving the initial help, but Natalie had made it pretty clear the festival was hardly on her radar. Now, Brody was swiveling in his seat, pointing to the fizzy drink he was promised. Whatever it took, Thad wanted to end the call and make the most of time with his son. "Ready, Fran."

He wrote down Natalie's number. Then Fran explained where Natalie lived, and she suggested Thad find out Natalie's correct email *when* he spoke with her. "Okay, Fran. Thank you. I hope you have a good night."

"You, too—" Fran cleared her throat once more, her voice growing hushed. "Natalie will most likely give you all this information at some point, so there's no need to mention the phone call."

Thad screwed his forehead at the strange request. "Uh, if I call her, she's sure to wonder. I'll just wait for her to offer her number, then."

"Dear, you are a debonair, successful young man. Surely you know the advantage of being mysterious with details. But if I must help you out, I believe her information is listed in my emergency contact file. Easy cover-up, don't you think?"

And not very ethical, Thad considered with a tight smile as if Fran was standing before him. "Happy Thanksgiving, Miss Fran."

"You, too, dear," she sing-sang, and the phone clicked.

Thad turned the ringer off on his phone and placed the paper with Natalie's info in the bin of unopened mail.

"Okay, Brody. First things first. Ginger ale and kickoff."
He tousled his son's hair.

"Can I pour it?" Brody was on his knees now, leaning
over the counter reaching for the bottle.

"Sure thing."

While Thad watched Brody unscrew the bottle, his
tongue poking out to the side, he soaked in the childlike
round cheeks, freckles and straight-as-a-board blond hair.
But more than the pure boyish looks, Thad was overjoyed
that Brody had settled in so quickly. No sitting on the couch
with his coat still on, as if he was counting down the minutes for Mom to come get him. The first few weeks in this
house were wrought with disappointment as Brody was
less than enthused about Thad's move. A stab in Thad's
already bruised heart. But tonight, Brody seemed to want
to be here. This weekend would be one more step toward
mending whatever gap existed between them.

Thad reached over to help Brody pour his drink. Brody
might never remember this night, but for Thad, it was the
best part of Thanksgiving. His hands engulfing his son's
little fingers as they tried to hit the cup and not the counter. Thad's chest welled with so much thankfulness, he
couldn't help but pray as their attempt to fill the cup was
not completely successful. Ginger ale pooled on the counter when they were done.

"No use crying over spilt milk." Thad chuckled.

"My teacher says that." Brody sipped his drink while
Thad grabbed the washcloth to wipe up the mess. "Mmm,
yummier than milk."

Thad poured himself some and helped his son down
from the stool to sit on the couch. "Happy Thanksgiving,
bud."

"Happy Thanksgiving, Dad."

Last year, Thad spent this holiday alone while Maxine

and Derek took Brody to Disney. Thad's living room was no match to a vacation, but for him, there was nowhere else he'd want to be. Rapid Falls was the best decision he'd made. And hopefully Brody would look back one day and agree with him.

Chapter Three

Natalie woke up on Saturday morning to soft whining and tail thumping beside her bed. Lex was within inches of her face, her big brown eyes round. She was hungry, no doubt.

"Okay, girl, I'm up." Natalie stretched her arms above her head. Her knuckles brushed the mahogany sleigh bedframe. Lex went from sitting to standing, her furry tail wagging.

She passed by the totes of Christmas decor that Dad had set out per Natalie's request. Mom had offered to decorate before Thanksgiving—a usual no-no in the Cooper household. Gigi would often insist, "Thanksgiving first, then Christmas season all the way through the twelfth day." From the day after Thanksgiving to Epiphany. But Mom was going to make an exception this year for Natalie. But as a loyal granddaughter, and a woman with little to do on her staycation, she insisted she'd decorate herself.

"Are you hungry?" Natalie took the sweet face in her hands and scratched behind Lex's ears. The dog's whole body moved with glee, then she galloped to the bedroom door, spinning around to see if Natalie followed. Natalie giggled and flung back the covers. This would be a great vacation if it started out with such happiness from her furry roommate, now watching her feet find her slippers.

Lex ate ferociously, then raced to the back door. While

she tromped around in the backyard snow, Natalie cozied on the breakfast nook window seat with her coffee and a slice of Mom's famous banana bread. She was surrounded by pillows and snuggled beneath a heavy knit blanket that colored most of Natalie's childhood memories with its burgundies, blues and golds.

After Lex was done with playtime, Natalie got ready and drove to the center. Gigi was bundled up, sitting in a rocker on the front porch beneath a heater. She never let the cold stop her, like most residents who'd grown up in northern Iowa.

"Good morning, dear." Gigi clutched Natalie's offered hand, rose from the seat and walked carefully to the car waiting along the curb.

"A beautiful morning, don't you think?" Natalie chimed.

"Yes, I do." Gigi patted Natalie's cheek with her woolen-gloved hand, and lowered into the passenger seat.

The drive outside town to the Vander Walt tree farm was shorter than Natalie remembered. And it felt a little strange partaking in this tradition without her parents.

After she parked in the small lot alongside the main farmhouse, they crossed the grounds to an open fire surrounded by Adirondack chairs. One end of a folding table was filled with baskets holding the fixings for roasting marshmallows and making s'mores. A large stainless-steel carafe labeled Hot Cocoa sat on the other end of the table. A little girl was filling up a disposable cup under the careful watch of an adult.

"What do you want to do first?" Natalie threaded her arm around Gigi's and squeezed her affectionately. "Pick a tree, or have some refreshments?"

"I think hot cocoa sounds nice. It's a bit chilly out here. Let's warm up." Gigi led them to the cocoa.

The smells of burning cedar and caramelizing marshmallows were perfect accents to this mild wintry day. Sunshine filtered through bare branches of tall cottonwoods and maples, while the distant rows of cedars, junipers and pine trees were being inspected by several young families bundled up in winter gear.

By the time Natalie had poured two cups of hot cocoa and added some whipped cream and cocoa dust, the chairs around the fire were taken.

"Sorry, Gigi. I should have found you a seat first." They stepped back and stood behind the nearest chair where a little boy sat with a roasting stick and a marshmallow ready to burst in flame above red-hot coals. He turned around and looked up at them.

"Hi, Mrs. Cooper." He smiled widely.

Gigi gasped happily, "Why, Brody! I didn't recognize you with that fantastic wool earflap cap."

Brody scrunched his nose and lifted his hand to the earflap. "Oh, is that what this is called?" His brown eyes widened with wonder, pushing up stray blond strands upon his freckled forehead.

Gigi laughed. "Yes, dear." Her bright twinkling blues boomeranged to Natalie. She stepped forward, expecting to be introduced, but Gigi all but turned her back to Natalie. "Now, where is your father? Or are you here with Mom?"

"Dad." Thad's deep answer carried from the other side of the fire. The retirement community director had transformed into woodsy lumberjack attire—the same coveralls as his parking lot attendant role, but he donned a red-and-black-plaid earflap cap, like his son. His teeth were white against a dark dusting of facial hair—a forty-eight-hour phenomenon emanating comfy-casual as opposed to clean-shaven professional. "Now, Brody, let's give these ladies our seats." Thad winked at Gigi, eliciting a flattered coo.

Natalie suppressed a laugh. But just as Brody and Thad began to rise, the other three seats emptied.

"You all stay," Gigi declared, tugging at Natalie's arm toward the empty chairs. "I was just about to say how much I miss your parents being here. This is second best." She returned a wink to Thad. Gigi sat in the chair to the left of Brody, while Natalie sat on her left. She introduced Natalie to Brody, then leaned toward the boy. "If only Lex were here, right, Brody?"

Brody gleamed and nodded enthusiastically.

"So, you all have been here before?" Thad rested his elbows on his knees while twirling a roasting stick, his marshmallow a pretty golden color. He sat directly across the fire from Natalie.

"It's a family tradition." Natalie smiled behind the rim of her cup. She sipped the warm chocolate drink while the fire crackled, the distant voices and laughter met her ears and Gigi's perfume faintly scented the cedar-filled air, just like old times. "The Vander Walts have been in the tree farm business since I was…" She slid her eyes past Gigi to Brody. "Probably your age. How old are you?"

"I am nine." He righted his roasting stick and observed his blackened marshmallow.

"That's burnt to a crisp." Gigi gaped at Brody.

The little boy wagged his eyebrows. "Exactly how I like it."

Everyone laughed, then Natalie continued, "Yep, about the same age as you, Brody. And I recall 'blackened' was my favorite kind of marshmallow back then, too. I was also a donkey in the festival pageant when I was your age. Nine is a very important age." She took another sip, amused by Brody's toothy grin. Her gaze knocked into Thad's steady stare.

Gigi asked, "And this is your first time at the Vander Walt farm?"

Thad dipped his chin. "Yep. We've never been to a tree farm before. Thought this would be a fun outing."

"The start of a father-son tradition?" Gigi added.

Thad grinned, his brown eyes now focused on his son. "What do you think, bud?"

"Mmm-hmm." Brody nodded with a mouthful of marshmallow.

"As far as I can remember—" Gigi turned toward Brody and said from the corner of her mouth "—and that's a long time." She chuckled then continued, "We've always picked out our tree. The scent of evergreen is a poignant reminder of the ever-present joy we receive from the Nativity." She let out a little sigh and sipped. Everyone turned their attention to the campfire at the center of their gathering.

Gigi set her cup down on her chair's arm abruptly. "Oh, that reminds me, Thad. It's also a tradition to have evergreen centerpieces at the Christmas Festival dinner."

He nodded. "I'll try and remember that."

Natalie's shoulders tensed, and by the look of Gigi's working jaw, she was thinking the same thing—*try* wasn't going to cut it when it came to tradition around the retirement center, or at least, around Gigi and her friends. "You know, Sally Grover sets up a pop-up boutique in the Vander Walt barn behind the house. Might be a good idea to put in an order today," Natalie suggested. Gigi's shoulders visibly lightened. Good. Natalie could do her part as adviser. That was much less stressful than planner extraordinaire. Although she had to tamp down the perturbed question— shouldn't there be a person in charge of the decor besides the retirement community's director? But asking that might give ideas that she would be up for such a task.

Thad lifted his roasting stick and began to slide off his

golden marshmallow between two graham crackers. "That's an idea." He seemed more interested in s'more making than the topic of the Christmas Festival.

"Why don't you show Thad the barn, Natalie dear?"

Thad paused midbite. "Oh, that won't be necessary. I'll find my way."

"I think it's a fantastic idea, honestly," Gigi persisted. "Natalie knows what to ask for, and well, it will be one more thing off your…plate."

"Dad, can we cut our tree now?" Brody piped up.

Thad rose as he bit into his s'more and skirted around the fire to Brody. Wiping the corners of his mouth, he addressed Gigi, "How about we see how the morning goes? I think the start of a tradition needs to fully develop." This time, his wink did not induce a flattered response from Gigi. Her smile only faded. "Come on, son. Let's find the perfect tree." He offered another bright smile, nodded at the ladies, then continued munching on his s'more as he followed Brody to the booth with tree saws.

"Hey, Gigi, let's go pick out a tree, too. The cocoa was perfect." Natalie laced her words with the most optimistic sweetness she could muster. By the perturbed hook of Gigi's lip, she worried that this year's tree cutting would be lackluster compared with all the happy memories in her mind. She rose. "I think a juniper would be best, don't you? No messy needles—"

"That's what we need for the centerpieces, too." Gigi held up her hand for Natalie to help her out of the deep seat of the Adirondack chair. "Don't forget, Natalie. Let's hurry so we can catch Thad before he leaves."

Hurry was not a happy word. It did not align with the Cooper tradition of sipping cocoa, strolling down rows of trees and taking impromptu family pictures when the sunshine cast a pretty glow on the winter-white background.

No, *hurry* was the word of Natalie's recent past when a bride was anxious to snatch up the last of the candle votives at a high-end boutique, or when Natalie rushed to arrange the guests just so in time for the great send-off of the newlyweds to their waiting limo.

The faint strain in Natalie's chest began to fill her thoughts… But fortunately, it was a fabrication of her mind, not truly present in her being. Yet.

"Gigi, if you promise to enjoy our time, I will make sure to get those centerpieces ordered. With or without Thad." Natalie wrapped her arm around Gigi's shoulder.

"Oh, dear, that would be wonderful." Gigi's shoulders relaxed. "Let's go find our tree."

Thad and Brody tromped down the row, commenting on the shape and height of each tree. Too narrow, too fat, not full enough, much too poky. But even though their inspection was playful and light, something nagged at Thad, as if the sharpest branch of the spindliest pine caught on his coverall, holding him back. The feeling grew stronger when, from the corner of his eye, he noticed the yellow stocking cap and short brown curls. Natalie Cooper and her grandmother were not far behind him.

Fran's insistent mention of the festival had put a damper on the warm conversation around the fire earlier. He would have much rather continued learning about Cooper traditions. Life had been so much about change these past few years. Thad had forgotten the comfort of tradition. Had he and Maxine established any at all? Thankfully, he was given this second chance to begin some new ones with his son. Maybe that's why talk of work irritated him today. It competed for attention, as work often had during Brody's young life. Not today. Giving Brody memories with his father was number one on Thad's priority list.

"Dad, look at this one!" Brody jumped up and down, his arms encasing the tall, narrow tree. "It's like a rocket ship! *Vrrrrooom.*" He crouched down, then shot up and called out, "Blast off!"

"So, is it going to land in our living room?"

"Nah. I don't think it will hold the decorations. You still have the paper chain I made in kindergarten, right?"

"Yep. Giant loops made of construction paper. Might swallow up this tree."

Brody nodded and crammed his hands into his puffy coat's pockets. They continued down the row, stopping at a few more trees, then finding the perfect one.

"Not too big, not too small." Thad stood admiring the tree.

"Round at the bottom and pointy at the top." Brody mirrored Thad by placing his hand on his hip, then added, "Just right."

Thad affirmed with a nod and knelt down, positioning the saw. Brody helped him saw back and forth, then called out, "Timber!" when the tree fell. They carried it to the front. Brody enjoyed watching a machine shake the tree for any loose debris. He helped a worker wrap the tree in netting.

"Our first Christmas present, Dad," Brody said as he stood with the tree beside him while Thad took a picture.

A worker suggested, "The barn has photo ornaments. A fave for tree poses like that one."

"Cool," Brody exclaimed. "Let's go get one."

"First, let's load the tree into the truck." Thad heaved the tree onto one shoulder, while Brody reached up and held onto the trunk.

"I'll help, Dad," he huffed as if the weight of the tree was pressing down on him. Thad's chest swelled with affection at his son's participation. Thad had a sneaking suspicion this was the first moment of a well-loved tradition.

After loading the truck, they headed back toward the barn. Natalie and Fran carried their tree along the edge of the parking lot. Thad jogged over to them. "You all need some help?"

"Why, that would be nice." Fran was out of breath and happily handed Thad her end of the tree.

"No problem." Thad and Natalie carried the tree the rest of the way while Brody and Fran waited by the fire pit. Once the Coopers' tree was secure to the top of Natalie's sedan, they all walked to the barn together.

"Well, look who Santa dropped off early!" A vibrant woman rushed over to them. She wore a wool poncho and giant silver hoop earrings. "The famous Natalie Cooper."

"Hello, Sally," Natalie gave the woman a hug. "It's good to see you."

"And you. Girl, I wish you could have come to my Black Friday social. I think you might have been impressed." She grabbed Natalie's hands. Sally's eyes sparkled like the Christmas lights twinkling from the rafters in the barn behind her. "Thankfully, I have two designers officing above the boutique. They offered their keen eyes."

Brody tugged at Thad's elbow. "Hey, Dad, they have trains." He pointed past the animated woman into the barn set up like an old-fashioned Christmas bazaar. A large aisle was lined with booths showcasing all sorts of festive goods. A delicious cinnamon-apple aroma stirred nostalgia in Thad's chest. He hoped to escape the chitchat while his son's excitement was still kindled. Standing with adults for too long would no doubt enlist Brody's usual bored shoulder sag. Short of keeping a ledger of successful Dad points, Thad was certain he'd stayed in the black this weekend.

He'd not risk losing momentum in this special newfound tradition.

He steered Brody back and around the gaggle, ushering him to the booth with a model of a miniature winter wonderland on a large table. A toy train zipped up and around on the impressive landscape model. When its whistle blew, Brody quickened his pace.

"This is pretty cool, huh?" Thad came up behind him as they both bent over to admire the scene. Brody walked along the front of the table at the same speed of the train, seemingly taking care to not touch the white felt material fashioned as snowy plains. "You know, this reminds me of the Christmas train my grandparents set up every year."

Brody stared up at him. "A Christmas train? Like one that goes around a Christmas tree?"

"Yep. I helped your great-grandpa set it up." He smiled at the rush of memories flooding his mind. He'd forgotten about the train set. "When I was your age, *that* was our first tradition of the season." He scanned the barn, trying to figure out where the delicious cinnamon-apple smell was coming from. "My grandma would make spiced cider that smelled just like—" Across the aisle, a U-shaped booth area was lined with shelves of jars and candles and paper sacks decorated with red-and-white-checkered ribbons. A chalkboard easel to the right of the booth was labeled Hudson Orchard Apple Goods. "Those candles, I suspect." Thad nodded at the booth, but his son's sole attention was on the long passenger train, as if he were peering in the windows for a glimpse at thumbnail-sized people.

Brody muttered, "Where's the train now?"

So, he was listening.

"Uh, that's a good question." Thad rubbed his neck. When his grandfather passed away, Thad had helped his father take inventory of his grandparents' estate. Surely, he kept something as special as the train. Unfortunately, Thad was in a difficult state of mind during that time—not only had the grief of losing his last and closest grandparent hit him particularly hard, but he and Maxine were finishing up divorce papers. Remembering details from back then was like trying to find the North Star in a sky filled with clouds.

"We've got a tree." Brody glanced up.

"I wonder if it's in my storage room." At that, Brody straightened and grabbed Thad's hand. "Let's go look."

Thad laughed at his enthusiasm. They were definitely related. He knew the anticipation of creating a rail system, no matter if it was all pretend. Thad pulled his keys out of his pocket just as Natalie and Fran walked over.

Fran patted Thad's arm. "Sally said she's got the centerpieces on display at her booth."

The anticipation crashed into his reality check. "Oh, yeah." He glanced among Brody, Fran and Natalie. "You know, you all have a better eye for that stuff. Why don't you go ahead and pick them out. I can pay for them first thing on Monday."

Natalie nodded and said, "That was my promise, right, Gigi?" Two faint dimples graced her rosy cheeks as she grinned at her grandmother. "I promised we'd get those centerpieces ordered, with or without—" She hesitated and glanced up at Thad. The yellow of her hat brought out the amber threads in her blue eyes.

Thad teasingly smirked and pointed at himself with his thumb. "With or without me? I appreciate the consideration."

Fran giggled, but the humor didn't reach her eyes, and Natalie bobbed an eyebrow in her direction.

Thad played it cool, chuckling and gathering his son to his side, then murmuring, "A train hunt awaits." Yet, irritation heated his chest. His old competitive self must be rearing up from beneath the warm and fuzzies of this winter outing. Natalie's admission of promising something with or without Thad hinted to an underlying jab at his own dependability.

Natalie smiled down at Brody. "Nice to meet you, Brody."

Brody turned a pleading look at Thad. "Let's go, Dad."

Thad squeezed his son's shoulder in fatherly affection. "Okay, son." Then he cast a grateful look to Natalie and swallowed his slightly bruised professional pride. "Thanks for helping."

Her smile tightened, and the light in her eyes dulled a little. She seemed annoyed, perhaps the same as Thad felt when he thought she had ignored his emails.

That was all a misunderstanding. Whatever she was thinking now probably had nothing to do with him. Maybe she was ready to go, too. But that Fran was persistent. And so was Thad's little boy.

Brody skipped ahead, then turned around and ran backward while calling out, "Come on, Dad. Let's go."

Thad shoved his hands in his pockets and began to jog toward him. This was an excellent start to the Christmas season. He prayed that he would find that train. If not, they might head back to Vander Walt's to purchase one.

Whatever kept this winning streak going with Brody, Thad would do it.

Chapter Four

After deciding on the ribbon and votive colors for the centerpieces, Natalie insisted on Gigi coming over for some of Mom's homemade chicken noodle soup—one of the treats Mom had stored in the fridge for Natalie's staycation.

Lex met them at the garage door, her whole body moving with glee.

"Ah, there's my friend." Gigi ran her hand through Lex's gold fur, setting off a tail wag that could knock over a bystander if they weren't paying attention.

But who wouldn't pay attention to such an excited ball of sunshine?

"I told you we'd be back by lunchtime, didn't I, Lex?" Natalie stroked Lex's back as she passed her to get to the refrigerator. "Maybe Lex would like to ride with us back to the center after we eat."

Gigi managed to get to the window seat with Lex at her knees. She lowered and continued to pet the dog, whose head now rested on her lap. "That would be nice. I wonder if Brody will be around."

"Does Thad usually come to work on a Saturday?" Natalie had her doubts. Especially since he and his son seemed to be enjoying the day together.

"No, I guess he doesn't. But he'll have to for the weekend of the festival."

"I think the burgundy and gold-trimmed ribbon is going to look fantastic with the gold votives." Natalie set the container of soup on the counter and pulled out a saucepan. She turned on the gas stove while Gigi cooed about the centerpieces.

"I am so glad you are here to help, Nattie. There are a million and one details. I'll get you a copy of the master list—"

"That won't be necessary, Gigi. I'd like to just help when I am around to do so." No strings attached. That would be best for Natalie. Otherwise, her ambition would take over, and she'd be back in the predicament of blood pressure checks and sleepless nights. She just couldn't cave to her persistent grandmother.

Gigi appeared vexed, her mouth sagging in a frown as she concentrated on her fingers threaded in Lex's fur. Avoiding the pesky details of Natalie's health situation was proving more difficult than she'd expected. Even so, she was determined to keep everything under control—her stress level and the perfect little staycation. A little consulting for the Christmas festival would not derail her plans.

Natalie focused on pouring the soup into the pot, stirred, then tapped the wooden spoon on the side and offered Gigi some ice water. "It's so strange to be here without Mom and Dad around. I'm glad you're close by."

Gigi looked up. "Huh, dear?" Before Natalie repeated herself, Gigi seemed to process what Natalie had said, and replied, "Me, too." Lex left her lap and tromped over to Natalie for her share of affection. "I am looking forward to playing cribbage, Lex's visits and your help." Gigi's shoulders heaved up with an intake of breath. "You will be around quite a bit, won't you?" She gleamed. "The retirement center needs a bright, energetic girl like you around this Christmas. Especially with Irene gone."

Natalie's chest filled with sympathy. Gigi was the last of her siblings alive. "Spending time with you is my number one priority, Gigi. But I don't know about my being energetic. My close second priority is getting some rest." There, she'd stated her plan clearly.

"The festival did so well last year. We were able to buy new appliances for the kitchen."

"Based on my own expertise, I am confident the festival will all come together." *With or without me*, she wanted to declare, just like she had about Thad earlier. Maybe she needed to share with him the necessity of his enthusiasm. If not for her own sake to guard herself, but for Gigi's peace of mind. "Rapid Falls is loyal to the retirement community—and the festival tradition."

The soup began to bubble. Natalie scraped the sides as she stirred. Rosemary-thyme-scented steam offered immediate relaxation like any comfort food should do. "Gigi, would you like to stay and help set up the tree? We can put on some Christmas music."

"That would be lovely, dear," Gigi chimed as she folded her hands on the table. It seemed the aroma had embraced her with its calming charm, too.

By the time they arrived to the retirement community, dusk had fallen on Rapid Falls, cloaking the naked tree branches and sloped roofs of neighboring houses with a gray veil. Burning firewood scented the freezing air in every breath—warming and chilling all at once. Unfortunately, the cold won the battle and Natalie, Lex and Gigi hurried into the lobby.

"Seems you have had help to decorate the place for Christmas," Natalie said as they walked past the living area. The Thanksgiving decor was replaced with fresh garland draped along the bookcases, mantel and side tables.

"That's Janet Hudson's doing. She does it every year when she drops off Don's mother after their family dinner at the orchard." Gigi rummaged through her handbag. She pulled out her apartment key.

"That's nice." As they approached the assisted living hallway, Natalie noticed the garland bows were frayed along the trim and the fake berries were chipped, exposing the white Styrofoam beneath their glittery surface. At first glance, the place shone with the Christmas spirit. "Are you all targeting the proceeds of the festival for anything in particular?"

"We'll figure it out after we get the numbers in. We hope last year wasn't the peak. Without Irene here, there was talk about a Thanksgiving festival so we could take advantage of Black Friday sales with the money we raised." She cocked her head toward Natalie and rolled her eyes. "Everything's more and more expensive."

Natalie nodded in agreement.

Gigi's apartment door was decorated with the quilted wreath that Natalie remembered as a child. "Aw, I love that wreath. And I remember the label from Great-Gran on the back." Natalie lifted the wreath to see the embroidered label by her great-grandmother's hand that read, *"For unto us a child is born, a savior is given."*

Gigi protested, "Oh no, dear, don't move—"

But Natalie had already lifted the wreath. The door's peephole had been covered up by the wreath. "Gigi, why are you hiding your peephole—"

Gigi's hand covered Natalie's to press the wreath to the door again. "It's fine how it is." Her cheeks were flushed, and she looked up and down the hallway. "I hang everything in that exact place."

Natalie narrowed her eyes. "Why? You can't see out of it then."

Gigi just waved a hand and unlocked the door. They stepped inside her room. Natalie suspected that Gigi didn't like the unsightly chipped and bubbled paint around the peephole. Natalie considered this because, if there was one thing she'd inherited from her Gigi, it was her attention to detail.

But the old paint job on the door wasn't the only detail that screamed for repair. After a thirty-minute visit in her grandmother's one-bedroom apartment, Natalie discovered the plumbing was dismal, the appliances were on their last leg and the most frustrating thing of all—the window needed repairing. Lex sniffed around a rolled towel on the windowsill used to block the draft.

"Gigi, you need a new room." Natalie sat down at the small kitchen table for two with a cup of hot tea.

Gigi set the kettle on a cool burner and tossed her oven mitt on the counter. "Dear, all the rooms have their quirks. It just comes with living in an older building."

"There are people called plumbers and repair guys." Natalie's tone was thick with sarcasm.

Gigi scoffed. "True. Thad has been helpful with that, at least. He's hired a great plumber. But one room at a time."

"Good, I am glad he's taking initiative." Natalie scanned the room, unable to take her eye off the drafty window. "What about the windows? That should probably be priority."

"Windows are expensive."

"But the company that owns the center should be able to replace them."

"I really don't know."

Natalie and Gigi finished their tea, but while Gigi filled her in on the latest Rapid Falls news, including the Hudsons' newest grandson, William Lance, Natalie grew more and more concerned about the condition of Gigi's apartment. Natalie Cooper couldn't just sip tea and ignore a problem that needed to be fixed.

The beloved residents of Rapid Falls Retirement Community deserved a lot more than a well-run Christmas Festival. It seemed they needed someone to advocate for them.

Natalie had never planned on being a spokesperson like that—especially if it called for getting up in front of people with any kind of script in hand. The thought had her reeling with dread, bringing up old, battered self-esteem. No, advocating for her grandmother and friends didn't require a press conference or town meeting. It only required a conversation. A one-on-one. She could handle that. And that's exactly what she planned to do first thing on Monday.

Thad greeted Monday morning with less enthusiasm than he had in a long time, only because he didn't want the weekend to end. These past few days were near perfect with Brody. Some of the best. As Thad passed the center's dining room, even the smell of bacon and cinnamon rolls couldn't distract him from the recent memories forming his lips into an unmovable grin. They had found Thad's Christmas train and set it up after decorating the tree. It may as well have been Christmas morning already. Brody had never been so excited under Thad's roof.

Thad unlocked his office door and flipped on the light. That pesky budget report sat on his desk, challenging his elated attitude. He was perplexed by how to help Rapid Falls Retirement Community thrive with such a tight budget. As he sat down at his computer, he opened up the grant application, finally allowing his smile to be overcome by business mode.

His cell phone chimed in his pocket. Maxine sent him a text. Her tone flung him back to in-person arguments when he was caught between coursework and her unmet expectations:

Are you kidding? Thad, Brody didn't finish his reading assignment. I thought you would parent this weekend.

Thad pressed back into his chair, running his hand across his newly cut hair. A groan escaped him as he positioned his thumbs on the screen.

I asked him if he had homework. He seemed pretty certain he didn't. Would you like me to email his teacher?

Thad stared at the message thread, waiting for a response, trying to replay his time with Brody by filtering out the fun and focusing on the several times he mentioned school. Well, it wasn't several times, but a couple of times on Sunday after church.

"Excuse me, Thad." Natalie stood at his door. Her short curly brown hair was outlined by sunlight from the window behind her. While he was dressed business casual in khakis and a button-down, she was sporting winter comfort— an oversize sweatshirt, leggings and fur-lined boots. "I'd like to speak with you a moment." Her glossy lips pursed tightly, and her blue eyes shone with intensity, deeper than the effect of perfectly applied eye makeup.

"I assume this is about some centerpieces. Did you happen to get an invoice?" He pulled his chair closer to his desk and set his phone down.

"I think Sally will email you the invoice. Actually, I wanted to talk with you about the retirement community." She eyed the chair across from his desk, so he gestured for her to sit, and she complied. "I am very concerned about the need for repairs, especially in the residents' rooms." The words came out perfectly sharp and precise, just like her posture now—back straight, leveled shoulders and her hands tightly held together in her lap.

"We are working on it, promise. The list is long, and the budget is tight."

"So, I suppose this year's festival is going to be the biggest and best?" Her passive-aggressive quirked eyebrow bristled Thad's nerves.

"A festival is not going to cut it, I'm afraid."

"Why not? The retirement community has always counted on it as their biggest fundraiser."

"According to last year's records, the fundraiser would need to bring in twice as much to help with repairs."

Natalie's rigid stance softened a bit, and she blew air from her lips, enough to lift a chestnut curl from her cheek. "That's a lot."

"Why do you think the director was shoveling the parking lot on Thanksgiving night?" He shoved a thumb in his chest. "I've been hired as the jack-of-all-trades, it seems." His joke fell flat on the concerned granddaughter's ears. "Look, I am trying to do what I can. I have a grant application ready to be written. The festival's nice, but it functions more as a tradition than the moneymaker we need."

"Well, the foundation's been laid—the tradition is well-known—maybe you all could amp up the festivities and get more cash flow. I know that our sister retirement community in Waterloo has some ties to loyal donors. Has an invitation been extended to our connections outside of Rapid Falls?"

"I guess we can send a second batch of save-the-dates out."

"Invitations would have been better than save-the-dates..." Natalie murmured, then shook her head. "Anyway, we need to send out more right away."

Thad slid his hands on his knees. "Don't you think it's a little late for that? I mean, most people have probably committed to plenty of Christmas events by now."

Natalie crossed her arms and hooked an eyebrow.

Thad raised a hand in surrender. "I know, Miss Event Planner. You know better than me." He conceded, although the pressure was on. "Susie Fredrickson helped mail the last batch. I am sure she will be willing to do the next."

"Good. She's reliable." Natalie thrummed her fingers on the chair arms. "We just need to offer something worth the drive to Rapid Falls."

"We?"

Natalie shrugged her shoulders. "I said I could help."

"Should I add you to the committee?" Thad's voice cracked, and he nervously chuckled. "Having a festival coordinator would be a lifesaver, Natalie. I will admit, small-town traditions aren't really in my wheelhouse."

Natalie opened her mouth as if to speak, but she only pressed her lips together in a thin line. She shook her head and focused on her hands in her lap. "I can't head this thing up, Thad. It's just—" Her conflicted gaze took him by surprise. While he had verbally pleaded for her help, her blue eyes shone with an unspoken plea as she nibbled on her lip. "I can offer some suggestions."

Thad leaned forward, planting his elbows on the desk. "Like roping in connections from a whole different community?" He softly chuckled. "Your vision is really admirable, Natalie, but I don't know how we can top whatever happened last year."

His phone rang and vibrated on the desktop. He answered it, holding up a finger to pause his conversation with Natalie.

"Hello?"

"Thad, I am here," Maxine said in a hushed tone.

"Where?"

"I am here with Brody's teacher. No need to send an email. But if you could come to the school, that would be great. We have some issues to discuss."

"Okay, I'll be there in five minutes." Thad hung up and spoke to Natalie. "I have to go… My son's school… Well, an impromptu parent-teacher conference, I guess."

"So, what do you think about the second mailing?"

"If you can get with Susie on that, I am sure she'd be happy for guidance. I just want to curb your expectations. Our committee is small. Three of us. We meet tonight. Why don't you come and pitch your ideas?" He pushed back his chair and stood, anxious to get to Brody's school. "And Natalie, with all your expertise, we'd appreciate your helping hand where you can."

Chapter Five

The Christmas jazz music pouring from the center's main sitting area speakers did little to help Natalie's nerves—even though the song, "O Holy Night," was her absolute favorite. She breathed in deeply. Her senses hitched on the coffee aroma coming from the complimentary muffins on the console table behind the couch. Gigi and Susie sat in the two armchairs on either side of the hearth across from the couch, both taking turns giving Lex attention. The fire flickered beneath the garland along the mantel.

"You've been gone a while, dear." Gigi straightened the cribbage board on the side table between her armchair and a straight-back chair for Natalie.

She took one of the dainty white coffee cups from the cafeteria tray beside the coffee pot and poured some coffee. "Oh, I just bounced some ideas off Thad."

"Really?" Gigi's voice went up an octave. Lex backed away from Susie and pushed her nose into Gigi's lap, her tail wagging ferociously. All three women giggled.

Natalie took care not to spill her coffee as she rounded the couch and sat down in the chair poised for Gigi's cribbage opponent. "Susie, you didn't happen to send the save-the-dates to Waterloo Retirement, did you?"

"No, I didn't think about that. We've always just sent them locally."

"Hmm, I am thinking we need a larger reach this year. Could you email me the file and I can have my partner, Lindsey, look them over? She's got an amazing eye and maybe we can spruce them up to entice folks to make the drive." Natalie pulled her phone out to text Lindsey a heads-up. "This year has to be bigger and better."

"Now that's the Cooper spirit." Gigi punched the air playfully, and Lex let out a short bark in approval. Natalie and Gigi laughed again.

Susie did not seem so amused. "I'll email you." Susie crossed her legs and leaned an elbow on her knee, turning her torso toward their small group. "Unfortunately, we are a little late in the game to expand our efforts. Even with you around, Nattie." She gave an apologetic smile.

A breathy laugh escaped Natalie's lips before she took a sip of the bold roast, and the handsome Thad MacDougall came to mind. He'd said the same thing. "It's never too late, Susie. Who's on the committee?"

"Yours truly, as of last week."

"Ah, that's it?"

"Darcie Tipton. She agreed to cater." Susie's hesitation to say the name was evident in her upturned brow and lowered gaze behind her glasses.

Natalie set her coffee cup on the table. She rolled her eyes and muttered, "Of course."

"Dear, is something wrong?" Gigi slid her feet away from Lex, who was now curled up on the oriental rug that boasted of maroons, golds and greens.

Natalie exchanged knowing glances with Susie, then straightened her shoulders against old hurt. She hadn't even considered Darcie all these years. Life had taken such a turn for the better since her days at Rapid Falls Middle School. But if anyone else recalled that time through Natalie's perspective—usually a tear-filled one back then—it was her mentor, Susie.

Susie dipped her head in a sort of permission to speak, so Natalie nodded. It seemed the understanding was mutual because Susie explained, "Darcie wasn't the kindest girl to our Natalie."

That's one way to put it. Natalie remembered being shunned and ridiculed when she ended up in remedial classes after her dyslexia diagnosis. And her best friend since kindergarten, Darcie Tipton, seemed to be the instigator of it all.

"It's no biggie now." Natalie waved a hand to dismiss the subject of their conversation and the silly discomfort in her throat. "I'm all grown up. And I would never…ever… repeat those middle school years again." Her laugh came out too forcefully to cement truth in her words. But it was true. She'd gotten over the hurdles and grew up into a dream career. Now as a successful adult, Natalie coped in the best way whenever dyslexia gave her fits—she had an awesome best friend and business partner. Lindsey took the weight of paperwork, public speaking and general black-and-white details. With Natalie's creativity and drive, and Lindsey's astute attention to logistics and fine print, they had a great partnership.

Gigi reached over and clasped Natalie's hand. "Darling, you've come such a long way. From braces to a knockout smile and credentials that soar far above a middle school gradebook." She winked.

Oh, Gigi. "I love that you have so much faith in me." Her grandmother had been living in Florida during most of Natalie's youth. Natalie wasn't even sure if her parents had mentioned Natalie's learning disability back then. Her shoulders tensed as another forgotten feeling crept across her chest. Disappointment. She remembered it in her father's face in that testing room. After all this time, she knew his reaction was just the initial shock of it all. Maybe she had felt some disappointment, too—in her heavenly Father—in the fact that she'd been allowed to struggle so much before the diagnosis. She was all right with God's plan, though, wasn't she? Hindsight was twenty-twenty in the very best way.

Whatever the reason for the wait until middle school to reveal her needs, everything seemed to have worked out nicely. Maybe swinging a little further to the successful side than might be considered healthy. But all that would work itself out if she listened to her body. And her doctor. And Lindsey.

"I believe Darcie would welcome any thoughts you have, Nattie. She's a chef and organizing the menu for the festival. I've joined in as a liaison for the residents recently, at the request of Fran." She warmly smiled in Gigi's direction.

"So, you'll have a friend in the room when you plan our next steps, dear," Gigi added, patting Natalie's hand, then adjusting the cribbage board between them.

Ugh. Suggest, not plan. "I was only—"

Lex yelped in her sleep, and everyone startled. Natalie was thankful for the distraction. Because she was getting tired of insisting that she wasn't going to plan an event on her staycation.

But there was one thing stopping her from the umpteenth admission that she'd not get involved—the fact that she knew what it would take to make it the festival of her grandmother's dreams. And Natalie was certain she had the experience to do just that, without going overboard. She'd prove her ability to take care of her health *and* dabble in planning. At the first chest pang, she would back away. Easy as pie—or Christmas pudding, to be perfectly festive.

Monday had lived up to its reputation as the worst day, as far as Thad was concerned. He closed out the files on his computer screen and glanced out the dark window. Only the snow-laden windowsill was visible through the glass panes. The day was almost over. And if Thad could cancel tonight's meeting, he would. Plopping down on his couch and watching a football game seemed a much-needed retreat from this notorious first day of the workweek.

The meeting with Brody's teacher and his ex-wife was like receiving a lump of coal early this Christmas. Brody's teacher wanted to explain Brody's mark of "IE" on his progress report for literacy. Insufficient Evidence. He hadn't proved that he was at grade level for reading or writing. The worst part was the fact that the meeting had been called right after Thad had patted himself on the back for a good parenting weekend.

Far from it. He'd been the fun dad, but not the responsible dad that Brody obviously needed. How often had he used his minimal time with Brody as an entertainer instead of teaching him to value schoolwork? The usual guilt of falling short in his role as a father soured his stomach.

Thad stood up from behind his desk.

Natalie walked by his office door and hesitated when their eyes met. "Hello. The meeting is in the conference room, correct?" She held a folder close to her chest and wore the same yellow knit hat she'd worn at the tree farm.

"Yep. I'll join you." He skirted around the desk, lifted the festival binder from the bookcase and met Natalie in the hallway.

As he turned to lock the door, she asked, "How'd your meeting go this morning?"

"Meeting?" Oh, yes, she'd been there when he had received Maxine's call. He shoved the key in the knob and locked it, then faced her. "It was a parent-teacher conference. I guess it was…informative."

Natalie smiled in a comforting way. "Brody's a great kid."

"He is. Must be if you can tell from a ten-minute s'more-making session." Now he genuinely smiled at Natalie.

"More like thirty minutes." She was barely up to his chin in height. Her hat was a little low on her forehead, pressing against manicured eyebrows and shading her big blue eyes. Thad was tempted to adjust the hat. Something he would do for Brody without thinking. But the thought of such a gesture would be unprofessional with a woman like Natalie, at best. Too forward for a practical stranger—beautiful as she was—at worst.

"Thirty minutes is about how long I'd like this meeting to go." Thad stepped forward and looked at his watch. "I assume you've written your suggestions down?" He flicked the corner of her folder.

"Better than that. I've compiled contacts and a mock-up save-the-date part two to be sent to businesses and surrounding areas."

"Wow, you had time on your hands since our conversation."

She bounced her shoulders in a nonchalant shrug and started walking ahead of him. "I have an amazing friend who's up to her elbows in babysitting her nephews. She was happy to help with a grown-up task like creating a new save-the-date."

"Too bad I got the wrong email address," Thad muttered mostly to himself.

Natalie giggled and glanced over her shoulder. "I probably would have shut you down, anyway. This is my staycation. I don't need to work. My biz partner, Lindsey, reprimanded me when I first asked for help…" Her sentence deflated into a quiet tone. She stopped walking, then spun around. "But you know, Gigi is persistent. And those repairs?" She shook her head and tsked. "Really, really needed."

Thad rubbed his jaw. "Believe me, I cringe thinking about the snail-like plumber we've hired."

A flicker of appreciation shone in Natalie's gaze. "I don't think it's too late to make the most out of this fundraiser. Besides, it is pertinent to make it at least live up to festivals past. Irene would expect it."

"Irene?"

"Gigi's late sister. She founded the fundraiser when I was in first grade, I believe. She was the activities coordinator here before retiring."

"Ah, now I see why Gigi is so focused on the event."

"Yep, but it is true that the town counts on it, too." She continued to walk toward the conference room at the end of the hall. "That binder you're holding is a lovingly crafted guidebook. Hope you've studied it. Probably part of your job description." She pulled open the glass door with one hand, swiped off her hat with the other, then disappeared into the room.

Thad slowed his steps and breathed in deep, although there was little relief in filling his lungs with such a sinking feeling at all that Natalie implied. The only time he'd ever felt this way was during the dream where he'd shown up to a class that he hadn't known he registered for, only to discover it was time to take the final.

He'd underestimated the expectations for this event—or at least, his part in making it a success. Thad's phone trilled from his pocket. It was Brody. He paused, unsure if he should answer when the meeting was about to start.

But how could he ignore his son to discuss decorations and invitations?

He turned away from the conference room and answered, "Hey, bud."

Chapter Six

Natalie bristled at the sight of Darcie sitting at the oval conference table. The woman's attention was on a clipboard on the table in front of her. She wore an elegantly trimmed jacket with a button-up blouse. A blond fishtail braid rested over one shoulder, and wire-framed glasses were perched on her slender nose. Natalie suddenly felt self-conscious in her comfy clothes. When the door closed behind her, Darcie looked up.

"Oh, hey there, Natalie." She straightened her glasses and folded her hands on the clipboard.

"Hi." Natalie gave a fake smile and lowered into the nearest chair before Darcie could fully take in her outfit. Natalie was as much of a professional as this woman, regardless of her attire. "How have you been?" She straightened her shoulders as she set the folder on the tabletop, and mirrored Darcie's folded hands.

"I'm good. Just going over the past menus to see what I can come up with to make this year extra-special." Her smile wasn't smug, was it? Natalie couldn't help but engage her super sense of reading gestures instead of tackling overcomplicated contracts. Darcie's icy blue eyes beamed from behind her glasses. "I'm thinking about offering some tapas-style platters before the dinner."

Natalie couldn't get a read on her. Was she actually just

talking business? Maybe Darcie had no recollection of their troubled past together. It was over a decade ago. And it was probably easier for Darcie to forget since she wasn't the one who felt like a squashed bug at the ridicule and cold shoulder. For the first time in ages, Natalie's eyes stung at the thought of those days.

Nope, this *was* business, and Natalie Cooper was an expert in business transactions. No matter her casual attire and her carefully managed learning disability, she could keep up with Darcie in these matters.

Natalie smoothed her hand over her folder and said, "I have a lot of experience with that type of spread at an event. Actually, the gala I just worked on hired a renowned Spanish chef in Minneapolis for his award-winning small bites."

Darcie's lips parted slightly, but quickly pressed together in a tight grin. "Great." She shifted her eyes to the door. Natalie followed her gaze. Susie walked in and Thad followed. When Natalie returned her attention to her ex-bestie, she noticed the woman was studying her clipboard again, without a smile, and with a brow crinkled in concentration.

"Hello, you two." Susie breezed by Natalie and squeezed her shoulder. She took a seat next to her. "Have you filled Natalie in on the food, Darcie?" Susie's smile didn't falter as she bounced her gaze between the two women. Natalie returned an easy grin to assure her everything was fine. If that's what Susie was wondering.

Darcie answered, "Yes. Natalie's experience is astounding, though. If any residents have attended one of Natalie's events, they might scoff at my small-town catering offerings." Her eyebrows bounced up in thick passive aggression. Not so passive. And not really aggression...but obvious hurt.

Natalie's stomach sank. Her effort to prove herself worthy of sitting at this table had gotten the best of her. Her business-savvy demeanor was giving way to an ugly insecurity to prove herself.

"I agree with your decision, Darcie," Natalie spoke quietly. "Tapas-style platters will be a fun treat."

"Thank you," Darcie said. "We have several to choose from, so I need to narrow it down. Thad, are you still up for Thursday night?"

Thad nodded. "Brody will be with me. He can taste-test the kids' menu." He swiveled his chair, facing Natalie and Susie. "Susie, you sure you can't make it?"

"Sorry, it's my granddaughter's piano recital."

"What about you, Natalie? Want to join us? Might be nice having the founder's grandniece choosing the dishes." His smile invited Natalie to let go of the tension that had roped her in at first glance of Darcie. She flicked a gaze at the woman. Darcie only hooked an eyebrow in question— the question having nothing to do with her competence, but an invitation to the restaurant. After unintentionally belittling Darcie's career, how could Natalie pass? That could appear pompous, even if declining would mostly be to keep an arm's length at getting sucked into planning. Dinner couldn't hurt. She needed to eat.

"Uh, Thursday sounds good." She smiled as genuinely as she could—to everyone at the table.

"Great. That's a plan. Now, why don't you share your suggestions with us." Thad leaned back in his chair and put his hands behind his head like he was relaxing by a crackling fire, not heading up a planning committee. Clearly, he was giving over the reins of this meeting to Natalie.

She opened her folder, pulled out the mock-up save-the-date and said, "I believe if we can get more folks through the door during the festival, we might have the opportunity to raise substantial funds. I think we send out an event over email, including more information than just a save-the-date. This will be a quicker way to get on people's e-calendars. Besides the event in email, we'll attach a digital file, too—great to printout for community bulletin-boards." Susie took the sheet and nodded in approval, then passed it on to Darcie, who gave a curt nod, too. "Also, I've gathered a contact list of small business owners that are open to advertising events. The Waterloo Country Club has a special newsletter for holiday events, for example. With the promise of excellence—in a children's pageant, substantial auction items and food—" she offered a kind look to Darcie, who in turn dipped her chin, not as curt as before, but with understanding at least "—we might attract some generous attendees." She picked up the spreadsheet. "I can email these files to the person who will take this on."

All eyes were on Thad as Natalie slid the papers to the center of the table. He dropped his hands and scooted forward. "Uh, that's great work, Natalie." He cleared his throat. She'd mentioned earlier that this festival should have been in his job description. Well, it wasn't. Yet, he'd already grown attached to the residents. Making a few phone calls and writing up an email to nearby towns wouldn't keep him working into the night. "Forward it to me. That's fine."

Susie exclaimed, "Wonderful. And I will get the knitting ladies to start reaching out to our friends in nearby communities. Nudge them to get those copies on bulletin boards right away."

Thad pushed his chair back. "Sounds good. Glad to have you here, Natalie." Short and sweet, that was what he wanted. Maybe he would have time to call Brody back before bedtime. His son had called to talk trains, making Thad even more anxious to end this meeting.

"Oh, Thad, have you gotten a hold of the community

theater's director? For the pageant?" Susie asked just as Thad pushed his chair back.

"Um, I have not. Dinner and an auction were more on my radar."

Susie pushed her glasses up. "Oh, the pageant is a must."

Natalie piped in, "Remember I told you about it at the tree farm this past weekend... I was a donkey?" She laughed but faltered when she seemed to catch Darcie's eyes. "It goes way back, is all I'm saying. It is very important."

"Okay, I'll be sure to call the theater director first thing in the morning. I did rope her into my initial planning email—" He refrained from looking at Natalie, who was probably skeptical of his ability to keep up with email. "I know she received it because she responded. However, she's been quiet since then."

"Did you send over the old script? I think she's waiting on that." Susie cleared her throat.

"Have you talked with her?" Thad's voice cracked. That feeling of being unprepared for a class caused his palms to moisten.

Susie nodded. "She's a dear friend. No worries, Thad. She's been working with an old student's copy. But she would like the director's notes since she was out of town for last year's."

"Will do," he said with confidence.

Natalie looked back and forth between his pen and his notepad in front of him. A not-so-subtle request for him to write a reminder down. Begrudgingly, he did just that. They moved on to discussing the centerpieces and some decor, then everyone stood to leave.

Natalie handed her folder to him. "Here you go, Thad. You can have the hard copies, too."

"Great. What other information do you want to include that will sell this to out-of-towners?"

"Do you have a list of donors for the auction?"

"Just a few. Sally's Boutique, Hudson Orchard and… I believe Jim's is putting together a fruit basket." He tucked the folder in his binder.

Natalie's sigh was audible. He looked up and caught her exasperated gaze. "Thad, there should be at least twenty items at the auction if we are trying to raise even more money. I wonder how much dust is on that binder." She folded her arms, seemingly inspecting the binder in his hands.

"Those are the folks I can think of. I have some more who've committed. Just don't have the list with me." He shifted his weight. "But since you know so much—" That came out as a challenge more than a sincere matter of fact. He pushed his chin up and managed to grin. "I mean that in the very best way—" He reached out and placed a hand on her arm, then withdrew it quickly. She wasn't a friend he was trying to assure. She was a…colleague? Consultant? Natalie lowered her eyes to her crossed arms. "I'd love to chat with you about other possibilities. Maybe at dinner?"

Natalie looked up, cocking her head in question. "Dinner?" Her cheeks pinked and she rested her teeth on her bottom lip.

"Yeah, you know. At Darcie's pop-up dining experience this Thursday?" His chest thudded erratically as a thought crept from the recesses of his bachelor mind—did she think he was asking her out? Nah, surely not.

Natalie's expression froze, then she narrowed her eyes. "Maybe. But I guarantee you there are past donor lists in that binder. No need to reinvent the wheel…even if we are trying to expand the reach."

Thad gripped the binder tighter, wrestling with the feeling of being completely inadequate. This wasn't rocket science. It was a small-town festival. But he certainly didn't give it the attention he should, and now he was being held accountable by this bossy professional planner. "Tell me again why you aren't willing to be a key player in this?" Thad did not feel the need to tone down his challenge. Not when she obviously knew her stuff but built a strange boundary of keeping her part as minimal as she could.

Natalie opened her mouth to speak, a flash of resentment crossing her ivory face.

Thad continued, "I mean, it seems to me that you are more entitled to this event than any other event you've planned. You are the grandniece of the founder, you've got loads of ideas, and you know the town like Santa knows the North Pole." He grinned at the comparison, but Natalie did not. She pursed her lips and narrowed her eyes more. "All I'm saying is, you are in the right place at the right time, Natalie. Please consider your part in the game." Thad's phone chimed with a text. He glanced at it. Brody was sharing the name of a hobby shop his friend gave him to buy paint to touch up the train. A smile crept on his lips. He was ecstatic to find grandfather's train that evening after the tree farm. And so was Brody. Thad loved that they had a love for trains in common.

"Excuse me?" Natalie lowered her head to catch his gaze as he peered at the phone. "My part in this really is none of your concern. You are the director. Not a teen that can't keep away from his phone for more than a thirty-minute meeting." She brushed past him, a floral scent filling his nostrils, confusing his senses on the season. Springtime blossoms in the onset of winter. Refreshing, yet unexpected.

Thad spun around. "I have more than—" The door shut behind her. He was going to explain he had more on his plate than a fundraiser. Grant writing, for one. Probably more practical than raising enough money from a town tradition. And maybe she wouldn't have been so quick to judge his phone use if she knew the only reason he paid it attention was because of Brody.

Heat traveled up his neck at her implication that he was acting immature. He tried to sort through the mess of emotions in his chest, but no matter how Thad justified it, there was one thing gnawing his heart so raw that he couldn't ignore it.

How had a near stranger like Natalie Cooper echoed the same sentiment as his ex-wife during their rockiest moments? Thad MacDougall wasn't a child—a teen. He was a grown man, trying his best to do what was right.

As he walked through the center, shutting off lights that weren't needed at this time of night, he tried to convince himself that he hadn't done anything wrong, no matter what Natalie Cooper thought.

Embers from the fireplace in the empty living area caught his eye. He crossed over to put them out before leaving the building. It was so quiet. Nobody was around. All the residents had retired to their rooms. He heaped ash on the remaining embers, then adjusted the screen to be sure it was secure. Thad noticed the missing caulk between the bricks of the fireplace and the wall. His eyes traveled up and around the room, suddenly noticing run-down elements like chipped-away paint, discolored carpet and frost forming on the inside of the windows.

So much repair was needed.

He understood why Natalie had come to him this morning. Especially since someone she loved chose to spend her golden years beneath this roof. He needed to respect that. The first way he could show his understanding was by trying a little harder at bumping up this festival on his to-do list.

Chapter Seven

When Natalie visited the retirement center over the next few days, Thad did this weird jack-in-the-box move—emerging from his office to clear up any animosity after Natalie's heated accusation, yet popping back into his office after seeing her laughing with Fran and the other residents over coffee or cribbage. How would he confront her without appearing defensive and petty?

Why did he care so much about what she thought, anyway?

Perhaps it was because she wasn't the first one on Monday to imply that Thad was not living up to expectations. The parent-teacher conference had been a wake-up call from his "perfect" weekend stupor. Thad couldn't count successes with Brody if they were only in fun and games. He needed to help Brody focus on schoolwork, too.

Usually, Thad would take Brody to dinner every Wednesday. But since Maxine had a late-night meeting on Thursday, Thad agreed to adjust this week. Supposedly Darcie's pop-up dining experience at the riverside restaurant outside town would impress anyone from nine years old to ninety-nine years old.

When Thad picked up Brody for dinner, Maxine practically shoved a book in Thad's hand and said, "He hasn't finished his reading assignment."

"Okay, on it. We have a thirty-minute drive to dinner." He tousled Brody's hair before they got in the car.

Snowy rolling hills contrasted with property lines marked by dark green conifer trees. The drive was especially breathtaking as the sun bled along the horizon. It was not even five o'clock, yet it would be dark by the time they arrived at the restaurant.

Through the rearview mirror, Thad noticed Brody staring out the window instead of down at his book. "Hey, bud, keep reading."

"Dad, I was thinking we could build a tunnel for the train."

"Is there a tunnel in your book?"

"No, but wouldn't it be cool?" He grinned at Thad through the mirror.

Thad chuckled and agreed with a nod, then said, "Keep reading."

Brody groaned and pressed his head back on the seat. "But it's soooo boring."

"How can a book about an adventure with talking animals and secret passageways be boring?"

Brody dramatically hung his head over his book.

Thad suppressed another laugh and kept his eyes on the road.

When they pulled into the parking lot of Café Lewis, he wasn't expecting the pop-up dining experience to be so literal. The restaurant was situated along the river, with a deck wrapping around one side to the waterfront. Along the deck, three translucent, faux igloos glowed from within. The structures reminded Thad of the domed botanical center in Des Moines, although instead of glass enclosing the framework, the igloos were constructed of a clear plastic.

"Whoa! Those are so cool," Brody exclaimed.

"We're going to eat inside one." Thad parked the car.

He smiled at the ingenuity of making use of patio dining during an Iowa winter.

"Will it be cold?" Brody fiddled with the zipper of his winter coat.

"Nope. Nice and toasty according to Miss Darcie. She said they each have a heater inside."

"Let's go!" Brody opened his door and hopped out, tossing his book on the floorboard.

"Wait. Did you finish the chapter?"

"Uh, no," Brody said.

"Brody, you've got to finish it. It's going to be too dark when we drive home."

"But Dad—"

Thad shook his head. "It's important, Brody. Bring it with you and you can tell all your friends you read in a glowing igloo." He winked.

Brody huffed and grabbed the book.

After they checked inside with the hostess, Darcie appeared from the kitchen. Thad introduced her to Brody.

"Come with me. Your private dining room is all ready." She smiled, and they followed her through the restaurant. She explained how her fiancé constructed the igloos after she pitched the idea to her boss, Café Lewis's owner. "I've been able to create some of my own things for the menu, instead of sticking to the established fare. One day, I plan on opening my own restaurant."

"That's great, Darcie."

They followed her through the patio doors to the deck. She unzipped an igloo, and once they were inside, she zipped it up behind them, explaining, "We have to be quick to keep the heat inside."

Four wicker chairs with cushions were set around a table. Glowing lanterns hung from the top of the dome.

"Make yourself comfortable." She grabbed a water jug

and glasses from a cart to the left of the entrance while Thad and Brody sat down. Brody inspected the structure, completely enthralled by the concept. Thad was pretty impressed, too.

After Darcie filled their water glasses, she unzipped the dome again to return to the kitchen. Just in time. Natalie approached.

"Oh hey, Darcie." Natalie shifted to the side to give Darcie room to exit.

"Welcome to Café Lewis." Darcie gave a quick nod. "Help yourself to some water. I'll be back with the first round of appetizers."

Natalie entered the igloo, closing the entrance before joining them at the table. "So, this is the most unusual taste testing I've ever been to." She took off her coat and set it behind her, filling the small space with a sweet blossom scent that reminded Thad of their last encounter.

"Glad you could make it." He smiled cordially. *My phone is tucked away, never to come out tonight.*

Natalie had wondered all day if she should cancel. After her snippy response to Thad in the conference room, she'd wrestled with embarrassment for first mistaking his mention of dinner as a possible date, and then being so quick to criticize his phone usage. But Thad had poked at Natalie's most prized possession—her moxie, her tenacious drive to make the most become even more. Thad had insisted that she should get more involved. Natalie would have never turned down that kind of challenge a year ago. And forgoing the chance to pour herself into a project like the festival… Well, that required an equal dose of self-control to her usual moxie.

For Natalie, obstacles had become challenges to try harder, press on, discover the way to excellence. She had first persisted through schoolwork, then starting her own business doing what she loved. Planning events wasn't just her job, it was her channel for creativity and accomplishment. A job well done was proof that her God-given talents had conquered her lesser qualities. Nothing could hold Natalie Cooper back—except that pesky blood pressure monitor. For the first time in Natalie's career, she was being forced to hibernate.

Of course, Thad didn't know any of that—but when he did challenge her to *consider her part in the game*, she kinda lost it. Okay, she really did lose it—especially when his phone seemed to be the distraction of the evening.

But tonight, she was happy just to be helping a bit. She looked around the intimate space and caught Thad's gaze. He was handsome as ever in this golden light. Amber flecks were evident in his brown eyes, along with lighter tones in his short dark hair. He thrummed his fingers on his knees, which were level with the table that was more a coffee table than a dining table.

"Catching up on reading?" she whispered, and nodded to Brody, who was hunched over a book in his lap.

Thad put a finger to his mouth, signaling the need for quiet. He moved to the chair next to her. His cool, pine-spice cologne added perfection to the cozy atmosphere. "Guess it will be the quietest taste testing, too." He winked at her. "Brody needs to finish his assignment."

"Don't worry, Dad. I won't be able to read." Brody closed his book.

"You have to."

"I keep reading the same thing over and over. I just… I need someone to read to me." He crossed his arms.

"Brody, you are in fourth grade. You need to practice independent reading." Thad leaned toward Natalie. "That's what his teacher said."

The entrance zipped open, and Darcie entered with a wooden butler's tray. "Here we go. Canapés. Several different cheese and meat options on various crackers and breads. I especially like the fig jam with goat cheese."

"Goat cheese?" Brody scrunched his nose.

Darcie chuckled. "Don't worry, Brody. I made a special selection for you. A few combos with chocolate spread." She set the tray on the table.

"As long as there isn't any cheese with my chocolate spread." Brody's freckled brow dipped up in question. Everyone laughed.

"Of course not." Darcie adjusted some of the crackers. "I think these will be nice to offer while everyone mingles during the silent auction bidding." She straightened, seemingly satisfied with her presentation. As she should be. Natalie was impressed. "Do you all need anything to drink besides water?"

Natalie declined. While Thad ordered a pop and Brody ordered lemonade. Natalie tried a canapé. "These are delicious, Darcie. Perfect balance of sweet and savory."

"Thank you." Darcie's voice seemed an octave higher. "That means a lot coming from you."

Really? Natalie turned her attention to Darcie, but she didn't look her way, only left the igloo once more.

"She must be impressed with you—like the rest of the town." Thad leaned over and picked up a loaded cracker.

"I highly doubt that." Natalie inwardly winced at the recent memory of her pride getting the best of her on Monday. "Darcie and I don't have a great track record."

"Oh?" Thad popped the cracker in his mouth. He chewed and bobbed his head in approval. "Wow, those are good." He adjusted the napkin in his lap. "Have you known each other a long time?"

"Yes, we were friends in elementary school. But we grew apart around eighth grade."

"Middle school is…" He shifted his eyes in Brody's direction and seemed to think twice before speaking again. He cleared his throat and said, "Not any easier than elementary… So Brody, you have to read."

Brody munched on a cracker, obviously not his first one. He had chocolate on the corners of his mouth and all over his hands. "Dad, I don't want to mess up my book. Can I go to the bathroom?" He wiggled his fingers.

"Sure. I saw it by the sliding doors to the main dining room." Thad unzipped the entrance to the igloo, and Brody brushed past. "You're going to read when you get back," Thad called out as he watched Brody enter the restaurant. Darcie was returning with their drinks. She handed them to Thad, then guided Brody to the bathroom. "Thanks, Darcie."

"No problem. Just keep that closed. I'll wait for him, and he can help me bring out the next dishes. An extra pair of hands would be great."

He set the glasses on the table, zipped up the igloo, then sat down and groaned. "I'm not any better at inspiring a kid to study than I am at planning a party."

Natalie reached over and picked up Brody's book. "I remember reading these stories. Or listening to them was more like it."

"So, I was wrong to assume he needs to read to himself?"

"I don't think so. I am not an expert, but I do know that not every kid learns the same way or stays on the same pace as their peers." And that was the crux of her past with Darcie. Try explaining that concept to eighth graders when everyone was trying to fit in and be the same as their peers.

"Well, supposedly Brody's teacher thinks his pace is not acceptable. But he doesn't seem to care about that book."

"Brody said he wants someone to read to him. Have you thought about audiobooks? That helped me when I was younger. I would read along with the narrator."

"Huh, I hadn't thought about that."

Darcie and Brody returned. They replaced the canapés with more dishes. Darcie explained her concept for the food, and they dug in after she left. Savory quesadilla bites and sweet salsa were exceptional.

Brody slurped his lemonade through the straw, then asked, "Dad, do you think we could make that tunnel for the train?"

Thad took a sip of his pop. "Sure thing— Oh wait, you have to get that assignment done."

"It's hard to read here. This is just too cool." Brody's smile was nothing short of a juvenile smolder—an obvious attempt to steer his father from academic talk.

Natalie bit her lip to avoid smiling and encouraging his behavior. Thad's chest heaved in a visible sigh.

"Hey, bud, how about listening to the book?" Natalie rummaged through her purse for her over-the-ear headphones.

"Are you going to read it to me?" Brody picked up the book to hand it to her. "I really want to get to the part with that horse on the cover."

Natalie pulled out her headphones and handed them to Brody. "I have an audiobook app on my phone. I'll just download that book and, voila—you can read along while you listen."

Brody narrowed his eyes. "Do you not want me to listen to your conversation?"

Thad chuckled. "I *want* you to finish your assignment

so we *can* build a tunnel for the train." At that, Brody stuck the headphones on.

Natalie found the book from her library's audiobook collection and downloaded it. She plugged the headphones in the phone. "What chapter are you on?"

Brody opened the book and held it up to show Chapter Three.

Natalie began the audiobook. "Be sure to follow along with the words. That helps your brain connect it all."

Brody nodded and started following along, his finger moving across the text.

Natalie flashed Thad a smile. "There. Maybe that will help."

Thad kept his eyes on Brody, as if he were waiting for him to look up. But the little boy just kept listening and reading. "I think it's helping." His gaze shifted to her. "Great idea. I might take credit with his mom, if that's okay with you?"

Natalie nodded and warmed at Thad's gracious smile. If she knew anything about this man besides his multiple roles at the center, he had a reputation of being a good father to his little boy. Gigi was worried about his investment in the festival, and he hadn't even arranged for the pageant details. He may not be an expert planner, but he was here, wasn't he? Sampling delectables when he could have canceled to keep his son on task at home.

Natalie shifted in her seat, crossing her legs and leaning on her chair arm closest to Thad. "Hey, I am sorry about the way we left things on Monday night."

Thad leaned back and folded his hands on his torso. "It took me by surprise, I'll admit that." His mouth hooked in the most adorable lopsided grin. "I'll step up my game on the festival, I promise." He paused the conversation and locked her in a determined gaze. "Why don't you want to take this on? Your expertise is exactly what we need."

Heat filled her cheeks. She ran her hand through her bobbed curls. "This is my staycation," she tried to say as nonchalantly as she could. But instead, it came out as if she was trying to convince someone—mainly, herself. "Imagine if you showed up to spend time with your grandmother, and her retirement center's director handed you a stack of tasks to do."

Thad nodded. "Good point." He sipped his drink.

Natalie slowly exhaled in relief. She didn't want to appear weak to anyone by admitting her main reason for keeping her distance. She pressed her hand to her chest, feigning fiddling with her necklace. No tightening, no drummed-up anxiety from this event talk.

Thad murmured, "But I'd probably consider if any of those tasks included a fantastic evening beneath glowing lanterns and good company." There went that dashing smile again. Thad's charm no doubt got him points during his interview—especially if a knitting lady, or two, was on the committee.

Darcie entered the igloo with one last tray and a clipboard. She hardly looked at Natalie as she sat in the empty chair across from her. They began to discuss the top three choices to have at the festival. Natalie tried to shove away the old need for validation and focused on the task at hand with as much graciousness and positivity as she could muster. But some of Darcie's suggestions on how to serve the various dishes would definitely not work.

As soon as the words "Based on my experience…" came out of Natalie's mouth, she witnessed an icy facade transform Darcie's happy demeanor. Darcie was adamant that she knew what she was doing. But Natalie couldn't back down. She knew better. She had a couple of years of experience under her belt, and she was no longer the inferior peer in the room.

"I beg to differ, Darcie. It really will be less effective if we expect patrons to carry around a plate while they bid on items. Make it as enjoyable as possible. No juggling acts."

Darcie clamped her mouth tight and jotted down notes on her clipboard. "We'll see" is all she said.

Thad crossed his legs and looked uncomfortable. "I think you've done an excellent job, Darcie. Since you're in charge of the food, it's your call. Don't you think it's all good, Natalie?" He volleyed her a question he'd already answered.

Darcie gleamed at Thad, but when she caught Natalie's gaze again, her smile fell. "I'll do whatever is best for the festival. I've always tried to do what is best for all involved. It's worked out great so far."

Was she talking about business or hinting to her warped perspective of when she completely shunned Natalie? Natalie wasn't going to prod that beast awake any further. She just gave a curt nod and sat back.

Darcie stood, signaling the end of their conversation. "I'll make the final menu and pass it on to you—" she clearly addressed Thad "—for final approval." She disappeared again.

Thad blew out a whistle. "If the food isn't spectacular, it won't be because we didn't try."

Natalie slumped in her chair. "It's going to be great." Natalie's heart was racing, and she had frustrated herself by nitpicking Darcie's plan.

"You and Darcie both make great points."

"Thanks for being so diplomatic. I promise, I am not such a bear when I'm working." She fluttered her lashes. "I am so excited that Darcie's offering an elegant alternative to last year's nacho bar. We just—"

"Don't have a great track record?" Thad repeated her phrase from earlier.

"I guess I feel the need to prove myself to her." Natalie's words came out before her guard was completely up. She didn't want to appear so petty. It may be too late, though, after the heated banter with her ex-best friend. "Old hurt has a way of surfacing in the most unattractive way."

"You'd be surprised that I actually understand you more than you think." He set his gaze on his son. "My greatest fear is being trapped by someone else's perception of me. Especially when I am fully aware of my past mistakes. Who wants to be held to those forever? Not me." His jaw worked beneath his shaven skin, and he stared in Brody's direction, but Natalie suspected he was lost in thought.

"Me, too. I've changed so much. Guess I'm trying a little too hard to prove it."

"Well, you have the whole town of Rapid Falls singing your praises, Miss Cooper." The warm light cascaded on his features in the most attractive way. "I think your effort to prove anything is unnecessary." He winked.

Natalie shouldn't be so flattered by this guy's encouragement. But after the fake igloo had grown particularly icy during her battle of the appetizers, heat swarmed her cheeks in appreciation.

"Wow, I can't believe he's still listening." Thad nodded to Brody, who had been curled up facing Natalie, cradling his book in his lap.

"Um, he's asleep, Thad."

Thad groaned. "Wonder if he's made any progress."

Natalie leaned over and turned the pages in the book. "He's well into chapter four." She sat back in her seat.

"Good. He was supposed to get through chapter three." He crossed his arms with a sigh of contentment. "Our work is done here." He winked at Natalie, then leaned over and helped himself to more food.

After they finished eating, Natalie said good-night while Thad woke Brody. Instead of going through the restaurant, Natalie used the deck stairs to the walkway by the front door. Tonight was nearly fun. And she felt slightly accomplished in the most unexpected way—helping out Brody with reading. Funny how she could glean from her school days and help someone now, at twenty-six years old. She recalled the verse Susie had given her in the thick of her struggles—*Suffering produces endurance, and endurance produces character and character produces hope.* Maybe she'd given some hope to Brody tonight. Actually, she was pretty sure she'd witnessed hope in Thad's countenance. A flood of joy washed over her, yet she couldn't ignore the stab of remorse for cheapening how far she'd come by her bitter encounter with Darcie.

Who'd have thought her roots would be so engaged when she'd grown such praiseworthy wings?

Chapter Eight

When Thad dropped off Brody and told Maxine that Brody had finished his reading assignment with the help of an audiobook, he suspected that she was trying to not appear too impressed. Her statuesque impression was an aggravating skill he recalled during old times of discussing matters of the heart.

"Oh, Thad?" Maxine called when he was halfway down the driveway. "Would you like to hang out with Brody on Saturday? We've got a full day of renovating the basement. He'll be bored." She implied that he would hang out with Brody like a buddy—a friend needed to entertain her son.

"Well, if hanging out means father-son bonding time, yeah, of course."

"Sounds good."

"I'll pick him up early. I wanted to try the pond at the edge of our neighborhood. Ice is thick enough to fish."

"I'll have his stuff ready."

"And have him bring his book. We'll get ahead of the assignments next week, too."

Maxine's statue superpower wasn't strong enough. Her mouth slightly dropped. Did he stun her? Thad was determined to partner in all aspects of Brody's life.

"Good night." Thad would continue to surprise her with his parenting success.

Too bad the person who deserved the praise in the first place was Natalie Cooper. He couldn't figure her out. She seemed nice enough—especially with Brody—but when it came to the festival, her persuasiveness on implementing certain details didn't match up to her persistence that she wasn't going to get too involved.

The woman was more conflicted about her role in the festival than Thad had ever been. But he tried to remember that she was invested in the community and the people who cared most about the event. Thad understood that kind of loyalty. Trying to manage the details of life while maintaining full devotion to the people who mattered most called for a tug-of-war between the brain and the heart.

Thad woke up just before the sun on Saturday morning, as he always did when fishing was on the schedule. He loaded up his truck with fishing gear, including an auger for the ice.

Brody took a while to get to the door. From what Thad could tell, he needed a little convincing to get off the couch and put his shoes on. A knot tightened in Thad's stomach. What would it take for his son to be excited to come with him?

Finally, they made it out to the truck. Brody scooted into the back seat, jerking the seat belt from its resting position, and shoving it into the buckle with a click. "Did you bring the tent?"

"Not this morning, Brody. We won't be out very long, and we'll hang out on the perimeter today."

"Ah, man. I love the tent."

Thad cast an apologetic look his way but smiled on the inside. Brody was looking forward to this more than he thought. Maybe he would grow to love fishing as much as

Thad did. A huge blessing as far as a fishing father was concerned.

Once they set up the gear just past a dormant stand of reeds frozen in their swampy bed, Thad used the auger and cut a hole. The local anglers' website was correct—about four inches thick.

Brody knelt and peered into the hole while Thad set up his fishing pole. "I think I see some, Dad. What are they? Trout?"

"No, probably bluegill. Come on, I'll bait your hook."

Brody scrambled to his feet and stood next to Thad while he prepared Brody's pole. His son was intently watching him work, and Thad wondered if this might be one of his top ten moments of all time. He'd never taken Brody fishing when he was little because it had been Thad's time to think and process the hard stuff of a crumbling marriage. Fishing had been his saving grace back then. But now, the chance to teach Brody the sport, and devote his fishing-thinking time to Brody-bonding time. Fishing lines and reels—the best tools for redeeming moments lost.

Thad helped Brody cast the line into the hole, then placed the rod in the holder. "Okay, son. Take a seat. And I'll start on mine."

Brody shuffled over to his stool but instead of sitting down, he hurried past it to the bank. He exclaimed, "There's Lex!"

"Hey, Brody—" But his son was running as fast as he could, kicking up snow at full speed, racing toward the golden retriever with no owner in sight.

Natalie gasped. "Lindsey! I need to let you go. Lex just took off." She held up the leash and realized the clasp was broken.

Lindsey's tone matched Natalie's panic with her final words. "Oh no— Okay! Just remember what I told you."

Natalie ended the call and started jogging down the shoveled sidewalk. "Lex, come!" Her fur-lined snow boots weren't cut out for running. The dog had raced across the neighborhood park and was now galloping toward the pond. Oh no. What if the ice wasn't strong enough yet? It was only the beginning of December.

In the distance, a boy appeared on the top of the bank.

Natalie revved up to a clumsy sprint, feeling like she was in a bad dream. "Please stop that dog!" she called. The child did exactly that, wrapping his arms around Lex. She knocked the kid backward into the snow.

Thad approached from the pond and waved. Brody was the dog's rescuer, his round face now being licked by Lex. Thad and Brody entertained her while Natalie slowed down to an appropriate pace for her clunky footwear.

"Hey, you two." Natalie was slightly out of breath. "Thanks for grabbing her. I was afraid she'd go through the ice."

Thad stood between the dog and the pond, while Brody held Lex in a firm embrace. "The ice is pretty thick now. I checked the anglers' website." He patted Lex's head.

"Good. The clasp broke on her leash." Natalie blew at a curl that escaped her hat. "Whew, I didn't expect to get quite that much exercise on our morning walk." She attached the leash to Lex's collar by tying it through the empty hoop and knotting it securely. "She sure does love you, Brody." Brody giggled as Lex licked his cheek again. "My mom said that you two had a special connection." A quick bouncing movement behind Thad caught Natalie's attention. A line yanked up and down at a fishing spot. "I think you caught something."

Thad spun around. "Brody, it's your pole." He strode down the slope. "Wanna come pull it in?"

"Yeah, Dad." Brody raced down the hill, halted at the water's edge, and carefully joined his father.

Lex jerked the leash and pulled Natalie several steps toward the ice. "Whoa, Lex."

Brody reeled in a small fish through the hole. "Cool!"

Lex's tail began to wag violently, and in one giant yank, she hopped down the slope. Natalie slid behind, falling on her backside.

Thad caught Lex before she knocked over the youngest fisherman. "Are you okay?" He cast a concerned look at Natalie. "I'd help you up, but—" He glanced down at the bundle of golden fur in his arms.

Natalie pushed herself up from the snow, fighting off the tears induced by the pain of falling so hard and fast. "I'm okay. I guess we won't be taking a walk around the park anytime soon. Too much temptation for Lex." She laughed weakly and brushed off her snow pants.

"Brody, why don't you release the fish back into the water, and we'll help get Lex back to the sidewalk."

"Okay," Brody complied.

Natalie guffawed, "You're telling me I went through all that and you're not even keeping the fish?"

Thad gave a hesitant grin and shrugged his shoulders while Lex squirmed in his arms. "It's too small to keep. Besides, the process is the best part." His wink set off an exhilaration that should only come from a strong cup of coffee this early in the morning. "Come on, I'll carry Lex up the bank to a safe distance." Natalie followed Thad to the edge of the park playground. "You got a good grip on the leash?"

"Yep." Natalie ground her boots into the two inches of snow on the ground.

Thad quietly spoke to Lex, "Be a good girl. There you go." He stroked her back as she became entranced by his attention.

"You've got a way with her, too. Must run in the family." Natalie was impressed more than she should have been. Maybe because the last guy in her life was not a pet lover. Her ex would often mention needing a lint roller on standby when they'd eat over at Lindsey's house—she had two dogs and a cat. Natalie should have taken that as a sign of incompatibility. She just assumed that he would grow to love Lex like every other person the family's beloved dog encountered. But the man hardly grew to love anything about Natalie—including her drive to succeed. He was too focused on his own gain to care anything about hers.

Now, Thad stood across from her, beaming with accomplishment—not for his own reward, but for helping her harness the infinite energy of Lex. "I suggest heading that direction." He gestured over his shoulder with his thumb, away from the pond.

"I agree." She giggled and started past him.

Thad caught her by the elbow. "Before you go, I didn't properly thank you for getting the audiobook set up for Brody."

"Oh, not a problem at all." Actually, *all* Natalie could think about was the man witnessing her stubborn event-planning mode. Lindsey's warning rang loud and clear in her head—*You can't just help with an event, Nattie. At best, you'll become the back seat driver of this Christmas Festival, causing all sorts of near wrecks with people you care about.*

She studied the sincerity of Thad's chocolate gaze, feeling the urge to match his gratitude with something a little more pride-squelching. "And I am…really sorry I got so…feisty?"

He opened his mouth to speak, but just shook his head and chuckled. "*Feisty* is a word for it." He reached a hand down to pet the squirming Lex, firmly tethered to the leash. Most of its length was wrapped around Natalie's hand. Her insulated snow gloves cushioned any pain from such a tight strap against her skin.

"That dining igloo nearly imploded with tension."

"Did you see me just land on my backside? Well, that's kinda how Darcie made me feel during a very difficult time in my life. We were best friends—and then we weren't. I guess we both feel like we need to prove ourselves to each other." Was that true for Darcie? She wasn't the one who was misunderstood and teased. "I guess I can't speak for her. But for me, old insecurity got the best of me on Thursday night."

Brody ran up to them, and Thad pulled him to his side. "I understand that more than you think." His voice was deep and soothing, like a peppermint latte at Sweet Lula's on Main Street.

"Can I hold the leash, Natalie?" Brody reached out his gloved hand.

"Uh—" She looked at Thad.

"Bud, if she got away from Natalie, then maybe it's not a good idea." Thad began to guide Brody back to the fishing spot. "Let's catch another fish, huh?"

Brody resisted and knelt beside Lex. "I'm done, Dad. Lex is more exciting."

Natalie giggled. "Sorry, I can't really disagree with that." But Thad didn't seem amused. He eyed the fishing stuff, rubbing his cheek. Had she spoiled their father-and-son outing? "I think it's best that I take Lex home. Why don't you all finish fishing, and then stop by my house for some hot chocolate? Brody can play with Lex in the backyard and not worry about her running off."

"That's a good idea," Thad affirmed enthusiastically then mouthed, "Thanks."

"We're on Boxwood. Third house down with the gray siding, red door and black shutters."

As they parted ways, Natalie second-guessed herself. Why was she inviting them over? It's not like they knew each other all that well. And this guy had seen her at her not-so-best, acting like the Grinch more than a collaborative workshop elf. She rolled her eyes at the kitschy imagery that formed in her mind, as if she was the star character of a 1950s storybook. Or more like the pesky villain, tossing aside peace and goodwill toward men—or more specifically, a good-looking director who hadn't completely grasped the magnitude of a small-town tradition.

"Come on, Lex. Let's hurry up."

Lex jaunted ahead as far as the leash would let her, then turned onto the sidewalk toward home. Even if Lex had run off, Natalie was certain the six-year-old dog would find her way home again.

Once back at the house, Natalie put away her hat, gloves and coat in the mudroom, while Lex sat on her hind legs next to the counter with the doggy bone jar, her big brown eyes steady on Natalie.

"I know, I know." She walked over and threaded her fingers through the soft golden fur on the back of Lex's neck as she reached her other hand into the treat jar. Lex spun around, now intent on every movement of the mini bone-shaped treat in Natalie's hand. The dog happily received the treat and loped around the kitchen counter to the carpet by the fireplace, her favorite spot to lounge. But a large tote was in the way.

"Oops, I need to get those decorations up, don't I?" Natalie hadn't expected the task of decorating her family home to be quite so anticlimactic without her parents here. She'd gotten the tree up and somewhat finished with Gigi last weekend. But the mantel was still bare, and the buffet table in the dining room hadn't been cleared for Mom's favorite decoration of all—her ceramic nativity set.

"If only you could help me out, Lex," she teased as she slid the tote to the other side of the hearth. "It's just no fun by myself." The red-and-white-striped stockings were sitting on top of the tote's contents, and the star stocking holders were boxed up just beneath them. "We'll hang them real quick. For our guests. But first—" Natalie turned on Dad's sound system and found the Christmas music station. "Can't do anything without accompaniment, can we?" Soft piano keys floated from the speakers. "Let's have ourselves a merry little Christmas, huh, Lex?" She smiled as she placed the stocking holders across the white mantel and hummed along with the instrumental music.

This was her favorite time of year. And that was something Lindsey didn't take into consideration when she tried to dissuade Natalie from getting involved in the festival planning. How could anything to do with celebrating this season be stressful? She rolled her eyes, thinking about her last-minute shopping spree the previous year, when their business was just starting off, and she had to carve out time to even think about gifts, as well as count every penny she handed over to the cashier.

She'd come a long way. Long enough to feel slightly justified in her effort to prove she had what it took to Darcie. Natalie pushed aside the first memory of her best friend pretending she didn't know who she was in the eighth-grade hallway.

Lex's super sense must have kicked in because she nosed at Natalie's socked foot, distracting her from her thoughts. Natalie nudged Lex's torso with her toe, and the dog rolled over on her back for a tummy rub.

"Just a sec." Natalie finished hanging the last stocking, then bent down and indulged the golden retriever.

"Okay, let's see." She stepped back to admire her quick decorating work. "Perfect." The festive touch of simply hung stockings matched the jolly music filling the room.

The first chords of "Silent Night" began, and ironically, the doorbell rang, sending Lex barking and running toward the door.

Chapter Nine

Natalie gripped Lex's collar as she answered the door.
Thad and Brody each had rosy noses and cheeks and watery eyes from the cold. "Welcome. You both can leave your
boots on the porch. Unless Brody wants to go around back
first. I have a tantalizing hot chocolate bar waiting, though."

"I'll have some hot chocolate." Brody shrugged his
shoulders as if he didn't really care either way.

Thad squeezed his shoulder, and said, "Good choice,
bud." They both took off their boots, then stepped inside.

"You can hang up your coats and snow pants in here."

Lex was the perfect attentive hostess, staying right by
the guys as they followed Natalie into the mudroom adjoining the kitchen.

Natalie went to the fridge and set out the whipped cream
and chocolate syrup. "I can't guarantee my hot chocolate
is any better than Vander Walt's, but I have all sorts of
embellishments to make it extra fun." She opened mason
jars filled with toppings. Mini-marshmallows, peppermint
bits, toffee bits, mini-chocolate chips and Natalie's favorite, cinnamon sticks.

"Whoa," Brody exclaimed as Natalie moved the tray
from the counter to the kitchen island. A silly grin bounced
his freckles, and he licked his lips. "I can put these in my hot
chocolate?" He picked up the jar of mini-chocolate chips.

"Absolutely. I suggest putting them in the bottom of your mug before pouring the cocoa—that way they melt, and you can stir it all together for extra chocolate." Natalie handed him an oversize white mug with gold snowflakes. "Oh, and you'll want to add a few more to the whipped cream to top it off." She winked at the little boy, who was already digging in with a spoon.

Thad finished petting Lex and approached the end of the kitchen island. He wore a crewneck T-shirt and faded blue jeans. His hair had just enough length to wear the effects of hat-head, sticking up in an unruly way. Natalie couldn't help but smile at his comfy-cozy look after seeing him mostly in business attire.

He echoed his son, "Whoa," as he inspected the large tray filled with toppings. "I am amazed you set this up in that short amount of time."

"Set it up just now? Oh no. This is the first treat to mark the winter season around here. And it stays filled all season long." Natalie giggled. "The Coopers are avid chocolate connoisseurs." She lifted a tin from the corner of the tray and handed it to Thad. "Especially drinking chocolate. It's thick and rich." Thad turned the tin in his palms and studied the label. "Lula, the coffee shop and bakery owner on Main, introduced me to this a few years ago. She travels to Europe quite a bit. Her family is in Greece and Italy." Natalie lifted another mug from the hooks beneath the cabinet. She handed Thad a red-and-white-pin-striped mug.

Thad filled his mug with cocoa from the silver container by the sink, then turned to the fixings. "This is impressive. Definitely gets you in the holiday spirit." He bounced his eyebrows at Brody.

Natalie reveled in the praise of such a simple setup. "Maybe we should have a designer hot chocolate bar at the pageant's intermission this year."

"Oh, that's an idea."

"I am sure Lula would be up for donating items for the cause. Planning to stop by there tomorrow."

"Great. See, this is why we need you, Natalie." Thad cocked his head and grinned at her. His hair sticking up, his face unshaven and the joy sparkling in his eyes tripped up Natalie's ever-planning brain and sent her chest all aflutter.

She looked away, grabbing a mug for herself. Her over-active appreciation for praise was short-lived as her mind avalanched with festival details. "You did contact the community theater director, didn't you?"

"Uh…yes, I did actually." Thad dolloped some whipped cream in Brody's cocoa at his quiet request, then reached for the peppermint chips. "Thanks to Susie for bringing the director by my office on her way to a knitting club meeting. Sounds like they've recruited kids from Saint George's youth group."

"Perfect." Natalie sighed. "Susie is the best. She's done so much for this town, and me." She poured some chocolate chips in her mug, added the cocoa, then began to stir the drink with a cinnamon stick.

"Not only is she on the board, but she plans great activities for the seniors. Did she inspire you to be a planner?" Thad and Brody took their cocoa over to the kitchen table. Brody scooted into the window seat, while Thad sat across from him in a chair.

Natalie joined them, sitting next to Brody on the window seat. Lex crawled under the table and lay at their feet. "No doubt. Susie mentored me all through high school. Actually, tutored." She leaned into Brody and said, "That's who suggested audiobooks to help *me* with reading." Natalie sipped her spicy cocoa. "I have dyslexia. So, I needed extra help."

"What's dyslexia?" Brody had a whipped cream mustache. Thad and Natalie laughed while Natalie handed him a napkin.

"It's a learning challenge. Sometimes it takes me a while for the words to make sense when I read. That's why audiobooks are a great tool."

"The one you gave me put me to sleep." Brody hooked a lip in annoyance.

Natalie feigned offense. "What? I used an audiobook credit for that one." She quickly laughed and said, "No biggie. How's the cocoa?"

Brody sipped loudly, licked his lips and said, "Pretty good," in an unassuming tone.

Thad chuckled. "It's better than pretty good to me."

Brody once again shrugged his shoulders. Natalie was beginning to see the shrug was a habitual gesture for the guy.

"So, are you ready to go outside?" Natalie asked. Lex immediately appeared from under the table at the mention of "outside."

Now Brody's enthusiasm shone in full force, and he answered with a definitive, "Yes."

Natalie moved out from the window seat, and Brody scooted along, then ran into the mudroom to get his snow gear on again.

Thad wiped his mouth with a napkin. "You know how to steal a kid's heart, obviously—chocolate, golden retriever playmate. I saw him spying that stash of candy canes by the front door, too."

Natalie sipped her cocoa again. "He's a sweet guy. I was a babysitter in high school. Kids are so much easier to get along with than adults at times." She winced, thinking about the difficulty in a few of their interactions. But there was nothing turbulent between them now. Only the happy, upbeat sounds of "Jingle Bells" from the speakers, and the rambunctious readying of a boy with a dog anxiously waiting to play.

Thad looked over his shoulder at his son. Brody was warming up to the idea that he would spend time with his dad on a regular basis. "He's slowly getting used to his old man."

Brody stomped to the front door. Natalie crossed over, opened the door, and held Lex while Brody retrieved his boots. "I'll just put them on out back."

"Good idea." Natalie shut the door and followed Lex and Brody back to the kitchen. She opened the back door and Lex raced through, nearly knocking Brody down.

Brody laughed more today than he had in a while. "Silly dog."

"Be nice, Lex," Natalie called out, grinning wide as Lex tromped through the snowy backyard. "Have fun, Brody. It's freezing out there." She shut the door and spun around, rubbing her arms. *"Brrrrr."*

Thad spied Brody through the window. His son fell to his knees and wrestled with Lex.

"Maybe you should get a dog, Thad. Seems to me, your son lights up most with Lex."

He nodded, dropping his gaze to his mug. "Not anytime soon. Still trying to figure things out. I can barely make it home in time for kickoff most nights." His mouth hooked into a grin, initiating a dazzling smile from Natalie, so unexpected that his heart did a little flip.

"Imagine the joy that would fill your house, though." Natalie's voice was soft. She held her mug in front of her lips, smiled again, then took a sip.

Thad shifted in his seat, focusing on the practicality of what she suggested. "Imagine taking care of a dog, a boy…

and a pageant/dinner/auction/town tradition that you've never witnessed before."

Natalie widened her blue eyes, pressing her hand to her mouth. "I almost spat my cocoa all over you." She laughed. "I understand it's a lot. But it's heading in the right direction. And Brody's going to love the festival, too."

"As long as Lex is there." Thad chuckled.

"Not sure if that will happen… But I need to show you something." She went to the living room, opened a drawer in the end table by the sofa and brought an album to the table. She turned a few pages, then landed on one. "Guess who?"

A little girl with face paint and donkey ears showed off missing teeth in a wide smile. Thad said, "Ah, the donkey."

Brody burst in the door. Lex raced in behind him and lapped up water from her nearby bowl. "Can I have some water, too, please?"

Natalie crossed the kitchen to a cupboard. "Brody, look at that album with your dad. Maybe you can follow in my footsteps and be a donkey at the pageant this year."

"Did you have lines?"

"Nope, just a bray or two."

"Okay," Brody said with utmost seriousness. He didn't seem to catch any of the humor coursing through Natalie's suggestion. Thad had, though. And he couldn't help but consider the truth in Fran gloating over her granddaughter. She was *delightful*. Cutthroat event planner aside.

Natalie handed Brody the glass and he gulped it down. "Lex and I are going to make snow people."

"Snow people?" Natalie hooked an eyebrow. "You mean, snowmen?"

"Not just snowmen though, a whole family. Come on, Lex," Brody said and disappeared outside again.

"He's comfortable here, I suppose."

"You're a great hostess." Thad dropped his gaze. The sinking whipped cream in his cocoa formed a little island in the middle of his drink. "Seems like there's an ocean between us sometimes. He grew up half his life without me around every day, and when he was little, I was consumed with graduate school. Have you ever looked back and realized the people you loved most were more in your blurry peripheral than your focus?" He glanced up from his drink. Natalie was staring at him, running her finger around the rim of her mug. Her heart-shaped face flowered with pink, and she shifted in her chair awkwardly. He chuckled nervously. "Anyway, if I seem stingy with this whole thing—" he pushed on the album between them "—it's because I just can't take any more time away from my kid than I already have."

"I understand more than you think," she spoke softly. "One of the most important things you can do is invest in Brody's success."

Thad's phone dinged. Maxine texted a reminder that Brody had homework. "We'd better get going. Homework awaits."

"Sounds horrible." She grimaced and closed the album between them. "Oh, are you taking Brody to Main Street's Jingle Week? It's a perfect chance to follow up with proprietors about auction baskets. In person."

"And I would take Brody to this?"

"Well, yeah. If he likes anything to do with Christmas cheer. Oh, and they'll light the City Hall Christmas tree at dusk on Wednesday, I believe. I plan on taking updated save-the-dates to each shop before the week kicks off so they can hand them out. As long as you're ready to commit to the additional offerings we'll have at the festival?"

"Actually, I had an idea for a fundraiser—a little more low-key than a festival, but maybe we could do both."

"We aren't getting rid of the fest—"

"I know, I know. I wouldn't do anything to upset the retirement community residents. Don't worry. But what if we had an ice-fishing tournament?"

"For a fundraiser?"

"Yes. We could collect an entry fee, and each fisherman could ask family and friends to sponsor him based on their time on the ice."

Natalie lifted her shoulders on a big intake of air. "That is so not the kind of event I am used to. I think we should wait and do that after the new year."

Thad pushed his chin up. "I don't know. Might be a way to get some of those men to come to the festival, too. I know my dad, for one, wouldn't have gone to a silent auction. But he'd have gone to the pond all day."

"And this is why you should have done more than you've done. It's too late in the game…" Natalie stood abruptly.

Thad held his hands up in mock surrender. "Hey, you're the one that's trying to make it bigger than it's been. Didn't you say it wasn't too late to shift gears?"

Natalie frowned and quickly grabbed their mugs. "Look, we need to stick to what people expect from a festival. That's the sure way of maximizing our efforts." She strode past him and rounded the counter to the kitchen sink.

"I wasn't finished—" He eyed his mug as she dumped the contents. "Never mind."

"Sorry." Natalie didn't sound sorry. She sounded annoyed. "Do you approve of the new save-the-dates?" She faced him with a hand on her hip.

"Uh, hadn't looked at them yet."

"Well, please do. We need to get them emailed and printed before Monday."

"Okay, boss, whatever you say—" Thad's phone dinged

again, and he was happy to release himself from Natalie's perturbed stare.

Maxine texted, Please let me know that you got this.

Thad texted back, Yep. Heading to do homework now. He pushed from his chair. "Got to go."

"I'll be around the center this weekend, so if you have any changes, catch me. Or text." Natalie turned on the faucet and rinsed out the mugs.

"We'll do whatever you think's best. For sure."

Natalie shut off the water, then faced him, narrowing her eyes like she was trying to decipher his meaning. "*Are* you sure?"

"Yep. I'll be at the retirement community's chapel service on Sunday. How about I confirm then?"

"Okay." Natalie wiped her hands on a towel.

Lyrics filled the silence between them, *I need a little Christmas, right this very minute*, and as Thad went to the back door to call for Brody to finish up, he let out a big breath of frustrated air. Thad was pretty sure the song meant a different kind of Christmas than this chaotic season was turning out to be.

What would it look like to help his son stay on top of his schoolwork and make up for all the lost bonding time, while juggling details with such a persistent creature as Natalie during this most busy season of all?

Chapter Ten

After Thad put on his snow gear and finally convinced Brody to leave, seeing themselves out the back gate instead of going through the house again, Natalie called for Lex, keeping the door open minimally, to prevent the cold from coming inside.

"Come on, girl." Natalie's command encouraged Lex to gallop the last few yards into the house. Clumps of snow trailed along the wood floor, while Lex waited at the treat jar once again.

"I am very confused, Lex." Natalie gave the dog a treat, patted her head, then began to tidy up the hot chocolate fixings. "I don't know whether to like Thad MacDougall or be completely annoyed with him."

He was handsome, fun-loving and lived up to the rumor that he was a great father. A sprout of compassion was firmly rooted in her consideration, knowing he felt distant from his son. But when it came to details of the festival, their ideas seemed to clash.

A fishing tournament? The guy really should have looked through her photo album. He didn't get it.

A muffled ring came from the mudroom. Her phone was still in her coat pocket. She fished it out and accepted Lindsey's call.

"Hey, Linds."

"Did you get her?"

"Huh?"

"Lex!"

"Oh, yeah! We got her." Natalie walked through the kitchen to the living room. She plopped on the couch and noted the perfection of her mantle decorating from earlier.

"We?"

"The retirement community director and his son helped me wrangle her."

"Oh, *Thaddeus*?" Lindsey said his name like a Shakespearean actor. "Seems you've been spending a lot of time with the guy," Her voice dripped with teasing insinuation.

"Not really, Linds." Natalie ran her socked toe across the edge of the coffee table, similar in height to the table in the igloo. "Well, yeah, I guess I have. But it hasn't been pleasant." At least some of the time. Sitting across from him drinking cocoa with Christmas music was just as cozy as their hor d'oeurves sampling. But both were short-lived. The only cozy time she should expect had to do with a big golden fluff ball, Mom's collection of throw blankets and a roaring fire.

"I've been meaning to ask. Have you been tracking your blood pressure?"

"Yes, Mom."

"Natalie, you told me long ago to keep you accountable. And both times we have talked, you've seemed pretty amped up about this festival."

"Don't worry, I have a good hold on it. All I have to do is put some things into play, and everything will work itself out. I am just the motivator, really."

"Oh, so you aren't making lists upon lists of things to do between now and the twenty-third?"

Natalie glanced over at the rolltop desk near the hallway. So, she'd made a few to-dos. "It's more of a brain dump than stress inducers. Besides, I passed off most of the stuff at the meeting on Monday."

"Good."

"There's something Thad said that's irritated me."

"Oh, what's that?"

Natalie grimaced as she remembered the look of defeat in his eyes. "Something about being so focused that his loved ones lost out." She picked at her lip, a wave of old emotion filling her chest. "Do you think I sabotaged my relationship with Harry? I mean, he's the closest thing I had to…the real thing, I guess."

"What?" Lindsey nearly screeched. "He was nothing near what you deserve. You were not a priority to him, Natalie. Don't second-guess."

"I know. He's a really good dad."

"Who?"

"*Thaddeus*," Natalie echoed Lindsey in the same thespian voice.

"Got it." She giggled. "So, I don't have to come down there and tie you to a cup of tea and a remote control?"

"You don't. I haven't had one tweak of tension pain. It's Christmas, after all. Brainstorming the festival is like dreaming of a white Christmas."

"Uh, looks like we've got a good chance of that up here in the great tundra."

Natalie glanced over at the window where Lex was peering out at Brody's snow *people*. Two were complete, and a third was headless.

"The festival is giving me thinking time on something other than hashing out the mistakes of yester-events." Too bad her encounters with Darcie flung her into yester-years.

Lindsey's voice was muffled as she spoke to someone else. "Hey, Natalie, I have to go. Duty calls."

After Natalie ended the call, Gigi texted.

See you tomorrow morning? The service begins at ten.

Definitely. Can't wait.

Regardless of Natalie's conflicting emotions, it had been nice to have people around today. She walked over and snuggled with Lex, observing Brody's snow people. Her staycation was becoming a string of events with a boy and his dad.

How could she stay annoyed with Thad for very long when he was the one person who'd stepped away from her peripheral and sat right in front of her, drinking hot cocoa and sharing his heart about his son? Even if she'd been assigned to keep tabs on the festival by Gigi, Natalie had to admit Thad was in full focus by default. And besides her blood pressure being a determining factor for her involvement in the festival, her last heartbreak was also a very real barricade to her heart's overactive reactions to Thad MacDougall. No use focusing on that slight inconvenience in her staycation, lovely as it was. She and Thad were in two very different frames of thinking. Come January she would be full-throttle involved in the next wedding, corporate event and a year's worth of other functions that would certainly make this staycation a blur.

The next morning was not a perfect-hair kind of day. The frustration of curly hair was peaking. No matter how much product she used, and despite her attempts with the curling iron, her hair was lopsided—curly on one side, and barely wavy on the other. She rummaged through the bathroom drawer, pulled out bobby pins and twisted her hair the way she'd watched many bridesmaids do. Upon finishing her half-up, half-down hairstyle, Natalie was lost in thoughts of the spring weddings awaiting in the new year until someone knocked on the front door.

Lex galloped away from the bathroom. As always, the dog was first to the door, and first to greet the outsider before the deadbolt was turned. Her barks echoed in the foyer. Natalie peered through the sidelight.

Thad met her gaze with an apologetic grin.

Natalie opened the door, smoothing down her knit dress that slightly clung to her tights. "Hey, Thad."

"Sorry to bother you. I was on my way to the retirement center and realized I didn't have my wallet. Haven't seen it since yesterday." He stepped inside, and Natalie shut out the biting wind. "Wondering if it might have fallen out in your mudroom."

"Oh sure, feel free to look." She waved an arm toward the mudroom. Thad slipped off his shoes on the foyer rug, as was custom to do upon entering any house during Iowa snow days, then managed to walk with Lex's close and personal escort.

"I've got to finish getting ready." Natalie turned to the foyer mirror to adjust a loose curl. She slid the bobby pin out from her hair and stuck it between her teeth, then twisted the curl into place again.

"Found it," Thad called, then spoke sweet words to Lex as he returned.

"Good." Natalie patted the sides of her hair and fussed with the curls brushing against her neck but not quite to her shoulders.

"Looks great."

Natalie spun around. Thad stood at the door, slipping

on his dress shoes, but not releasing Natalie from his gaze. His attentive brown eyes had her melting at his compliment. "Oh, my hair? Thanks," she said, knowing full well that he was just being kind because she was primping in front of him. "It's being extra stubborn this morning." The grandfather clock chimed on the three-quarters of the hour. "I'm going to be late for the service."

"Want me to drive? We're going to the same place." He ran his fingers along the periwinkle dress collar beneath his clean-shaven jaw. Lex jumped up on him, and Thad instinctively caught her by the sides, jostling the dog playfully. "And you won't be allowed to drag the pretty lady through the snow today." His dashing smile was meant for Lex, but Natalie felt overwhelmed by his sincere flattery. She managed to contain a modest smile and slipped her feet into faux suede pixie boots.

Thad gave a final pat to Lex then glanced at Natalie. "So, want to go together?"

"Sure." Natalie ran past him, into the mudroom, trying to ignore the addition of a spicy and appealing cologne in the air. Why was he affecting her like this? Was he trying to convince her to take over the festival with his charm and good looks?

Natalie smirked at the thought, knowing it wasn't true. Thad MacDougall was too caught up with worrying about time with his son, which was an excellent excuse for his laid-back attitude toward the festival. Natalie shook her head… Such an attitude toward the beloved Christmas event was unfathomable to her. Not swoon-worthy behavior at all. Besides, Thad was a handsome family man who'd never approve of her all-in love for work. She'd dealt with that disapproval before, and it held her back. Never again. And she convinced herself of that the entire walk down the sidewalk as Thad gently pointed out slick spots, offering an elbow.

Not swoon-worthy one bit.

When they arrived at the center, Thad took their coats to the coatroom while Natalie met Fran and escorted her to the chapel. He was impressed with the turnout. Besides the residents, young families filled the room to watch their children sing at the end the service. The last time the chapel was this full had been on Veterans Day when they held a special family service for the many retired military members who resided here. Thad found a place to stand behind the back row of seats. Two men stood beside him after giving up their seats for Fran and Natalie.

During the intermission between the service and the preschool performance, chatter filled the room. The Saint George's preschool director gathered the children to form a line at the back of the center aisle. Thad introduced himself to her since they'd spoken on the phone earlier in the week.

"Nice to finally meet you in person, Mr. MacDougall." Jane offered a hand for a shake, even though she was bent over, adjusting a little girl's bows on her pigtails.

"You, too, but please, call me Thad." He had reiterated that on their phone call, as well.

"Will do." She straightened and led the children down the aisle.

The kids sang "Away in a Manger," "O Little Town of Bethlehem," "Hark the Herald Angels Sing" and, finally, "Silent Night." All was calm, all was bright as the many family members beamed and videoed their children.

Thad walked up after the applause and faced the crowd, his gaze snagging Natalie's as if she were the only familiar person in the room. Not true, but a sense of comfort overtook him. Aftereffects of her hosting and listening ear yesterday? Most likely.

"Thank you to all the parents who agreed to worship here today. I am sure I speak for all the residents that this was a very special treat. The Christmas spirit is alive and well at Saint George's, don't you agree?" The audience applauded again. "Please join us in the dining room for some refreshments. All the preschool families will find a table with their name and a gingerbread house for their children to decorate." Excited voices bubbled from all the children standing behind him on the risers. A ripple of laughter went through the room. Thad hurried out of the way as preschoolers were escorted to their parents.

Natalie joined him as they left the chapel and headed to the dining room. "I don't recall this being a thing last year."

"Hey, I have ideas, too." He winked at her. "This was one of my favorite Christmas memories from Brody's younger years—a program and family gingerbread decorating."

"Is Brody here?"

"No, although I wish I invited him. Would have been fun to see him decorate a gingerbread house now. We couldn't stop him from eating the candy when he was three."

"You mean you aren't supposed to snack while you decorate?" Natalie feigned surprise. "That's the best part about gingerbread houses if you ask me. Kinda like fishing."

"Like fishing?" Thad stopped walking and turned to her. "You've got my attention now, Miss Cooper."

She just continued walking, talking over her shoulder, "A wise father once told his son that the process was the best part—of fishing. But I think it's the same for anything involved with candy decorations, too."

Thad shouldn't feel so pleased that she remembered his off-the-cuff encouragement to Brody at the fishing hole, but he couldn't help it. It wasn't often that someone acknowledged a positive takeaway from his time with Brody. Mostly, he was alone with his son, sometimes feeling more like a floundering fish than a knowledgeable father. Maybe his words meant something to his son, too.

Thad followed Natalie into the dining room. A little girl plowed into him, wrapping her arms around his legs. "Hello there." The same little girl with pigtails from earlier had already lost a ribbon and now peered up at him. "You're not Mr. Sean." She grimaced and backed away.

"Ava, we're over here." A tall blond-haired woman called across the room. She stood with Natalie and Sean Peters, the landscape architect whom Thad had met during some maintenance in the center's gardens.

Ava ran full-speed into Sean's legs. "Ava, you were awesome." Sean laughed. He reached out to shake Thad's hand. "Hey, Thad. This is my soon-to-be niece. Ava, this is Mr. Thad."

"Ah, *Mr.* Thad. A new name for me." Thad winked at Natalie only because she was the person he knew best. But he didn't mean to activate such a deep flush of color in the woman. Sean then introduced Thad to his fiancée and the girl's aunt, Elisa, and Ava's older sister, Lottie.

Natalie cleared her throat. "Sean and I were in high school together."

"We hardly see you around here," Sean said. "I heard business is booming for you."

"Let me guess, knitting club talk?" Natalie's dimple appeared with her playful grin.

Elisa and Sean laughed, exchanging knowing looks, then Elisa said, "Marge suggested we talk with you about our reception. We want a sweet garden-style party in my backyard. Do you have any experience with that?"

Suddenly, Natalie's face went from teasing to full-on

excitement. She began to share about her last outdoor wedding. "Why don't you email me?" She dug through her purse and pulled out a business card. "Are you all looking for a planner or consultation? I'd be happy to do either."

Thad was amazed by Natalie's willingness to work. Her passion was obvious. While Thad was trying to manage his work-life balance, that woman was itching to start in full throttle when it came down to her own work. He was tired just watching her. The slow pace around here suited Thad just right. He reserved his energy for raising a boy to become a man. As long as he could prove that he was capable of such a task. Seemed each time he tried to spend time with Brody these days, Natalie showed up, pushing the festival details his way.

Seeing her now, though, Thad was perplexed. Event planning seemed to really excite her. Why did she resist getting too involved in organizing the festival? Especially since she was so connected to this community.

Thad caught her eye as Sean and Elisa left to help Ava get situated next to her older sister, the gingerbread house between them. Natalie exhaled and pressed her hand to her stomach as if she'd stepped away from a tricky situation.

"Are you okay?" Thad walked beside her as she made her way to the back of the dining room.

"Yeah, I just promised myself no work talk." She quickly looked up at him. "Strange to talk shop on my staycation, you know?"

"Not really. You seemed just fine, until…now."

"I am fine. Just surprised myself, that's all."

"You surprised me, too."

"How so?"

"Well, you've been pretty adamant about not planning this festival. I guess a backyard wedding is more enticing."

Natalie's mouth dropped. "Excuse me, but drumming

up business for the spring and picking up the slack around here on my time off are two very different things."

"The slack? Hey, I was willing to make it nice and simple this year. There was no slack, just…streamlining."

Natalie let out an exasperated laugh and opened her mouth to speak. But Fran joined them, and the event planner's heated glare shifted to an attentive gaze to her grandmother.

Thad adjusted his tie. "Hello, Fran. Did you enjoy the program?"

"It was wonderful," she exclaimed, placing her hand on his arm. "Susie told me it was all your idea."

Thad nodded, resisting a peek at Natalie. Was she impressed that he could plan an event too? Why did he care what she thought? Maybe it had something to do with how beautiful she was when she spoke to a potential client. To have that kind of reaction directed toward him? Thad swallowed hard, ignored the skitter in his chest, and gestured to the coffee and pastries on the buffet table. "Can I help you all get some refreshments?"

"I think we can manage." Natalie's tone was syrupy sweet, and she threaded her arm with Fran's. "Come on, Gigi. Let me tell you about the Hartley-Peters wedding."

Chapter Eleven

Natalie and Fran joined a few ladies by the fireplace in the living area. Susie Fredrickson and Tina Delaney sat on the couch, and Marge Webber and her daughter and preschool director, Jane Barlow, sat on the love seat.

"Marge, you made my favorite. Orange cranberry muffins." Natalie set her plate on the small table between two armchairs.

"Darling, it's good to see you." The spritely Marge sprung from her seat and opened her arms. "Why haven't you come by Lula's yet?" She embraced Natalie.

Gigi piped in, "She's been busy with the festival planning, haven't you, dear?"

Natalie pulled away from the rose-scented air that marked Marge's presence and offered a tight smile to her grandmother. "Hardly. Only giving suggestions." She sat in her seat and began to peel the wrapper from the muffin. "I hope to come by the café tomorrow morning first thing, Marge. Lula's peppermint latte has been calling my name for about eleven months now."

Everyone laughed and began to chat about all the happenings around Rapid Falls. And so much was happening. The community was vibrant with active citizens. Especially this time of year, during Main Street Jingle Week. But Natalie was distracted by Thad's insinuation that she was held to some double standard, and worse, that he may have implied her loyalty to work outweighed her dedication to the retirement community.

Natalie despised being misunderstood. Half her life seemed to have been a series of misunderstandings—first when she was younger, and her parents took her poor grades as her lack of trying. But then in her teen years, when her friend group thought she was defective because of leaving class to get help from the reading specialist.

Actually, the way others saw her, and evidently talked about her, convinced Natalie she had been defective for quite a while. Especially after the betrayal of Darcie Tipton—the one friend she'd spent nearly every day with the summer before eighth grade—and the one person who stopped talking to her altogether the next fall. Everything came crashing down once Natalie's adjusted school schedule seemed to label her as abnormal among all her high-achieving, suddenly silent friends. A wise woman helped her through it—Susie. Natalie caught the woman's eye and offered her a warm smile.

"Dear, would you hand me my purse?" Gigi pointed to the handbag at her feet. "I need to take my medicine."

Natalie set the bag on Gigi's lap. Her grandmother pulled out a long pill box with compartments for each day of the week. Natalie suddenly remembered she'd forgotten her blood pressure medicine two days in a row.

She gathered up her half-eaten muffin and untouched coffee. "I—I'd better go tend to Lex."

"So soon? You haven't finished, dear."

"I'll come back this afternoon." She stood and kissed Gigi's cheek, then said her goodbyes to the group.

After disposing of her refreshments, she hurried to the cloakroom. Where did she hang her coat? Her mind was slipping.

Oh wait. She arrived with Thad. Natalie groaned at realizing she didn't have a way home except—

"Hello, Natalie." Darcie's greeting was soft.

She spun around. "Oh, hello."

Darcie glanced into the cloakroom behind Natalie. "Did you get your things?"

Natalie was blocking the entrance, so she stepped aside. "Excuse me, you go ahead." Darcie slid past. Their coats were hanging beside each other. "So, you're leaving now?"

"Yes, it was a cute program." Darcie slid on her peacoat. "My nephew was in the choir. Heading to my parents' house now." She fished her keys out of her pocket.

Natalie reached for her own coat, feeling awkward after their last encounter. But they were here now, grown up and successful. And Darcie's parents lived around the corner from her. And… Darcie's keys jingled from her finger in suggestion. "Um, can I ask you a favor, Darcie? Could you give me a ride home?"

"Uh, sure." She glanced down and fiddled with her keychain. "Did you not drive?"

"No. I got a ride with Thad. But who knows how long he will take."

"Thad?" Darcie's tone and obvious amusement mimicked Lindsey's reaction once *Thaddeus* became the topic of their phone conversations.

Natalie explained hastily, "We ran into each other, and since we were going to the same place at the same time… I just got a ride." She shoved her arm in her coat sleeve.

"Okay." The last syllable lilted upward as if she wasn't completely convinced. There was absolutely nothing to defend. Was there?

Natalie followed her out, tightening her coat belt with one hard squeeze. She walked beside her former best friend to the car, second-guessing the need to be punctual with her medicine-taking. But her current and ever persistent bestie's voice filled her thoughts with a command. *Take your medicine!*

They passed by Elisa Hartley's remodeled Victorian. Natalie had only run into Sean and Elisa a couple times since they'd gotten engaged. Their design office was above Sally's Boutique, one of Natalie's go-tos for event center-piece inspiration. Natalie tried to catch a glimpse of the backyard as they passed, wondering about the reception she might plan. They drove by too quickly. She turned to the very quiet and focused Darcie behind the wheel. "Have you seen the backyard since Sean finished it? I wanted to go on the tour of homes, but I had a wedding in Des Moines that week."

"A whole week for a wedding?"

"So many details to manage, and a very high-maintenance bride."

"It's beautiful—the backyard, I mean." She turned on her signal as they approached Boxwood Street. "The yard is terraced, with sweeping flower beds and a unique struc-ture at the center. Oh, and her nieces have a state-of-the-art playground area."

"Sounds great. I'm already dreaming of the reception."

"You're working their wedding?"

"I am not a hundred percent sure, yet. We're going to meet and discuss."

Darcie just lifted her chin up. A gesture of understand-ing or defensiveness? Natalie wasn't sure.

The rest of the drive was silent, and Natalie was relieved when they pulled into her driveway.

"Thanks, Darcie." Natalie reached for the door.

Darcie turned her whole body toward Natalie, and planted her forearm on the console between them. "Look,

I've talked to Sean and Elisa extensively about catering their reception."

Natalie's hand slipped from the door handle. "Okay?" She was confused by Darcie's obvious frustration. "I'm an event planner, not a caterer, Darcie."

"I'm just saying I'd like to have first dibs—even if you have your repertoire of award-winning caterers." Her manicured eyebrows dipped with determination, but her lip quivered. Natalie hadn't interacted with this woman much, but she understood the expression on her face. Feeling threatened by the competition. Yep, Natalie understood that feeling very well.

Natalie cleared her throat. "I don't know that I have a repertoire... But would you really want to work with me?" Natalie wasn't so sure she wanted to work with Darcie any more than the woman seemed to want to work with her.

Darcie looked away. "It makes no difference to me."

"Good. Then don't worry about the Hartley-Peters wedding." Natalie sighed and again reached for the door.

"It's been really difficult seeing you this time around." Darcie fiddled with her steering wheel. She continued in a soft voice, "I know that you didn't think it was a big deal, but I had a hard time when you kind of dropped me in eighth grade."

Natalie's jaw fell like a broken Nutcracker doll. "You mean when *you* dropped *me*."

"I did not." Darcie grimaced. "You suddenly went radio silent—kept to yourself. You didn't even tell me why you switched out of the one class we had together."

Did she really care?

Natalie searched her mind for clarity on all she remembered. Everything was...blurry. "All I know is, I was stuck in remedial classes and you seemed to think it was a fun topic to joke about with your friends."

"I did not, that's just not—" Her lashes fluttered as she ran her hand through her long blond hair. Darcie propped her elbow on the steering wheel and faced Natalie again. "I may have—I guess. I can't remember. I just know I was so hurt when you stopped talking to me."

"I thought *you'd* stopped talking to me." But Natalie began to wonder if maybe she hadn't communicated as much as she could have. Did she say anything at all when her schedule changed? If Natalie had learned anything over these two years of building a business, it was her ability to appear completely fine even if she was struggling. Lindsey finally convinced her that she wasn't okay when she kept experiencing lightheadedness. Physical effects were hard to hide. Emotional effects were much easier to conceal. "I guess I didn't want to say the truth out loud. And then, after I had to drop my electives, word was out about my dyslexia, and you seemed just fine with a new group of friends."

"I couldn't believe it when I heard. But you seemed pretty adamant you didn't want to talk about it. I guess I should have stood up for you." Darcie shook her head. "It was middle school. Survival of the socialites, right?" She rolled her eyes at her poor joke.

Natalie managed a smile. "I am so glad middle school is over."

"Me, too. I am really sorry that I didn't stick up for you. I know it was a long time ago, but I was hurt that you chose to not tell me about your diagnosis. I was your best friend. I guess my teenage brain didn't know how to respond to the rejection."

"All this time, I thought you rejected me—" Natalie leaned against the car door and pressed her hand against to her forehead as a slight headache began to throb. "Because of my learning disability."

"I didn't care about that."

Only the hum of the engine filled the space, but there was no igloo-like tension or unspoken judgments. Just a settled calm. Communication was a very good thing—and long overdue. Darcie broke the silence with a quiet laugh. "Obviously you overcame your remedial classes Miss Event Planner."

Natalie grinned. "And you've become a rock-star chef. We've both come a long way, huh?"

Darcie nodded. Her blue eyes sparkled with relief. No hesitation or animosity.

"Thanks for the ride, Darcie." Natalie opened the car door and stepped outside. "I am glad we talked."

"Me, too." Darcie tucked her hair behind her ear and gave a small wave before Natalie left.

As she headed inside, Natalie tried to recall any memories of her middle school days that gave clues to what Darcie shared. Even though she couldn't think of any, she was certain that her old best friend was sincere. She said a small prayer, thanking God for clearing up the misunderstanding. Her dad's kind eyes and wide smile gleamed from a family portrait in the foyer. They were more like home than this cozy house *almost* decorated for Christmas. Yet, back when she'd first received her diagnosis, Dad's eyes had dimmed a little. Natalie's memory was *not* mistaken. Especially since she had overheard a conversation between her parents, and although she couldn't remember most of their words, what she did remember had made her feel like a disappointment back then.

They'd said one thing that Natalie couldn't forget.

Where did we go wrong?

Her learning disability was a disappointment to the two people she loved most.

Thankfully, she didn't keep quiet with her parents like

she had with Darcie. They were very quick to correct Natalie's thinking. They had been confused and tried to make sense of it. Most of all, they apologized for their wording. And Natalie was assured, for the most part. Although, she didn't want anyone else to find out about her diagnosis. And holding it inside grew her insecurities like a snowball gaining speed on a downward slope.

Lex greeted her by nosing her thigh. Natalie knelt down. "Missed you, too, Lex." She wrapped her arms around the dog and grounded herself to the present. Seemed like a good time to call Mom and Dad and check in. She pulled out her phone and noticed a text from Thad.

Where are you? I'm ready to take you home.

Ugh, she'd just learned a lesson about communication, hadn't she?

Sorry, needed to get going so I got a ride.

Natalie headed to the bathroom and opened her pill bottle. Earlier, Thad had no idea that Natalie's chest tightened slightly while she spoke with Elisa Hartley. Sure, her excitement for the project outweighed a silly stress pang, but still, if Thad had known about her blood pressure, she wouldn't have to keep resisting his plea for her help. He would stop asking.

Maybe Thad was the one person she could tell, because he wasn't family who'd grow concerned, or a client who'd view her as unreliable. He was *Thaddeus*, a guy who kept showing up on her staycation.

The next day, Thad and Brody headed to Main Street Jingle. He had only been to the business district a handful of times since he moved to Rapid Falls in July. Besides City Hall and a couple of lunches at the Rapid Falls Diner, he didn't have much reason, or desire, to go to the shops and boutiques. However, after meeting Marge and Lula during the retirement community's Thanksgiving preparation, he made a mental note to visit their café and bakery.

Tonight, there was no vehicle access to Main. Traffic attendants, with Santa hats, used light-up candy canes to direct cars to a vacant lot a block away from the downtown area.

Brody craned his neck up, trying to peer over the dashboard from the back seat. "Are you sure you won't get stuck, Dad?" The anxious crinkle in his forehead grew deeper by the second.

"Yep, they cleared it. Look at that John Deere tractor with the plow attached." He pointed to the back of the lot where a massive mound of snow stood higher than the machinery. "This is where they want us to park. No worries." Thad's stomach twisted once again witnessing Brody's anxiety kick in.

He prayed tonight would be all fun. No mention of schoolwork. Thad wanted to give his son some of that Rapid Falls tradition that everyone seemed ever allegiant to.

Natalie barged into his thoughts. The woman was unbelievable in more ways than one. Besides her ability to entrance him with her vibrant eyes and quick wit, her hyperfocus on the festival she refused to head up was mind-numbing. Especially after seeing her light up at the chance to work on the Hartley-Peters wedding. He was utterly confused by her mixed signals. Although, he wished his intrigue to get to know her better would grow numb so he could be satisfied with a purely professional relationship. He didn't need another woman in his life telling him he was falling short. Maxine had shoved Brody's homework folder in his hands at pickup, giving Thad a not-so-confident look that he could manage things. She'd also informed him that the audiobook win must have been a fluke. Brody was still distracted and struggling even though she'd bought a subscription for audiobooks.

"Let's go, Brody." Thad opened his door, hopped out, then helped his son down from the back seat of the truck. "Be sure to stay warm." He zipped up Brody's coat over the bundled scarf around his neck, offered his hand, and they followed a group of families to the sidewalk.

Once on Main Street, they approached City Hall, where a large crowd stood in front of a two-story window. Inside, a shadowy unlit Christmas tree nearly filled the entire window.

The historic building was decked out for the holidays. Garlands wrapped around the railings along the steps and accessible ramp. Two large wreaths with red bows hung on the wooden double doors, and a couple of decorative vases contained miniature Christmas trees with twinkle lights and ribbon that matched the bows on the doors.

"I can't really see anything, Dad." Brody pressed in closer to Thad, jumping onto his tiptoes and trying to peer between the people in front of him. Nobody stood behind them, so Thad offered Brody to get on his shoulders.

"Really?" The boy's face flushed. "Am I a little old?"

"I guess if you can ask that question, maybe you are." Thad pushed aside embarrassment that he was unaware of some father-son code. When was the last time Brody sat on his shoulders? He remembered trips to the zoo in Des Moines between his graduate school semesters. Surely that wasn't the last time? Brody had only been four.

"Maybe I am not too old." Brody seemed to inspect the crowd around them. "I see some kids on shoulders. Okay,

Dad, can I?" He threaded his gloved fingers together, and his eyes lit with anticipation.

"Sure thing, bud," Thad said nonchalantly, even though joy threatened to burst his heart at the seams. Something about his son trusting him, his shoulders, his strength, while brushing aside social anxiety gave Thad assurance that no matter what he had failed to do in the past, he had gained his son's trust right now. Sure, his offer was a simple means to watch a Christmas tree lighting, but Thad didn't care. He was the one person who made it possible for Brody to see the lights. To catch the beauty of celebrating light and wonder and the nativity of another Son who was loved by His Father, too.

Thad hooked his hands on top of Brody's boots that were level with his chest, and they listened to the Carol of the Bells grow loud over two large speakers standing on either side of the double doors. At the perfect swell of music, the massive tree was lit with what seemed like a million twinkle lights.

"Wow," Brody exclaimed, along with hundreds of *oohs* and *aahs* from the crowd.

"Pretty spectacular." Thad tapped his boot.

"Yeah, Dad."

The music changed to a jolly instrumental of "We Wish You a Merry Christmas," and the crowd started to disperse along Main, beneath old-fashioned streetlamps decorated with evergreen sprigs and red and gold bows.

"I'm ready to get down now," Brody insisted. Thad reached up and held Brody's underarms while the boy pulled his legs from Thad's shoulders and slid down Thad's back. "What should we do now?"

Across the street, Thad spied a glowing neon coffee cup in a window beneath a sign that read Sweet Lula's Café and Bakery. "Let's go get some hot chocolate and cookies."

"Okay, but I doubt it's a hot chocolate bar like Natalie's."

Thad chuckled. "I doubt that, too. But she mentioned it being pretty good."

They crossed the street and joined a line forming along the sidewalk.

"This is a long line, Dad."

Thad read a chalkboard easel. "Looks like they are giving away samples for Jingle Week while we wait. Should we stay?" Just then, Marge appeared, squeezing through the doorway with a round tray pressed up against an apron over her thick wool sweater. Her dyed-blond hair stuck out on either side of a reindeer headband, and her red lips seemed to match the festivities. She was enticing each person in line to sample her mini cups of drinking chocolate.

Thad nudged his son and said, "Brody, that's the stuff Natalie told us about, remember?"

"Natalie?" Marge echoed the name as if she was part of the conversation. Her bright gaze locked with Thad's. The older woman strolled up to him. "Did you say Natalie?"

"Uh, yeah——" He shifted, trying to appear completely unaffected by all the attention of the patrons who were probably wondering if "Natalie" was some code word to get to samples faster. "She was telling us about the drinking chocolate."

Marge looked down at Brody, scrunching her nose with pleasant acknowledgment, then returned her attention to Thad. "Dear, she grew up on the stuff. You two try it. But don't tell me what you think." Marge winked, a flash of mischief crossing her sparkling blues. "Tell *Natalie*." She giggled. Thad lifted his hand, waiting for her to hand the samples over.

"Tell me what?" Natalie stood behind them in her signature yellow knit hat, a yellow-and-black-striped scarf and no sign of frustration from how they'd left things yesterday. Perfectly glowing, as if she were in competition with that tree across the street.

"Oh, dear, thank you for spreading the word about our drinking chocolate." Marge reached out and squeezed Natalie's arm. "You join these two in line. Enjoy." But Marge turned away without giving them a sample at all.

Brody looked up at Thad. "Dad, we didn't get anything to enjoy."

Natalie narrowed her eyes playfully toward the back of Marge's platinum blond head while she said, "You don't know about the knitting club's favorite pastime, do you, Thad? It has nothing to do with knitting, and everything to do with matchmaking." She crossed her arms and called out, "Marge, of course we'll enjoy the company, but how about some samples, too?"

Marge swiveled around. "Oh my, I am a little distracted. You two are just adorable together." She handed over the samples. Thad's throat was thick with embarrassment, and something else…anticipation.

Chapter Twelve

Natalie couldn't believe she mentioned matchmaking to Thad. Sure, that was Marge's motivation—without a doubt. But Natalie didn't have to actually say it. Now, it was out there, lodging the idea in Thad's head, forming the question that Natalie couldn't stop from materializing in her own brain. She slung back the warm drinking chocolate and closed her eyes. Yet, thick, velvety, and cocoa richness was not enough of a distraction now. Could she see herself matched up with this man? Not in a business agreement, but in a romantic, full-fledged match, bearing the stamp of knitting club approval?

Thad didn't even look at her. First, he drank the drinking chocolate, his eyes growing wide in Brody's direction.

Brody licked his lips. "That was yummy."

"Sure was," his father agreed, following the line of people to the door of the café.

"Told you two it was the best." She breathed in the cloves and cinnamon that filled the café air. Her nerves finally settled into the cozy cheer of Sweet Lula's at Christmastime.

In rare fashion, Lula was mingling with customers instead of stocking pastries or making batches of her beloved Greek cookies.

"Lula, you've grown," Natalie jested when the four-foot-something Greek woman gave her a hug.

"New shoes. My daughter took me shopping." Lula's rolling accent carried over the bustling café chatter. "Look." She nodded down to her feet and turned her boot to show a chunky heel. She leaned closer. "Tell me the truth, do you think they are too young for me?" She was probably the same age as Gigi.

"Not at all. They look very nice with your black pants."

Lula gave a satisfied nod and adjusted her burgundy knit sweater. "Thank you, Natalie." She continued moving along, greeting Thad, who introduced Brody.

Once they received their orders, they went back outside. Music played from the speakers by City Hall, and people strolled along the brightly lit sidewalks. They stopped by a few of the businesses, mainly to make sure the save-the-dates were displayed, but also to allow Brody to partake in the various complimentary treats.

The diner was set up like a workshop. The old-fashioned soda counter was reserved for children to write letters to Santa. After Thad convinced Brody to participate in the activity, Thad and Natalie waited toward the back of the crowded area next to the to the back door.

"This is a little quieter here." Thad swirled his cup, then tipped it back to finish off the last of his caramel macchiato. "How long has Jingle Week been around?" He tossed his empty cup in a nearby trash can.

"Hmm, as long as I can remember. It's pretty fun, huh?"

"A great tradition. Glad I got to experience it with Brody first." Thad watched his son for a second, then squared his shoulders to face Natalie. "Seems like we've spent a few of these Rapid Falls traditions with you, too. Are you certain you are just an event planner and not some Christmas elf sent to bring us cheer?"

Natalie giggled, pushing down the bubbling enthusiasm for this private conversation in the midst of a crowded space. They may as well have been the only two people in the room—and she didn't mind it one bit. "You'll soon realize that participating in Rapid Falls events is never done solo." She took a sip of her peppermint latte, luscious and invigorating as always. "I appreciate you all letting me stick with you tonight. I usually walk this event with my parents. Although, last year I missed it entirely."

"What happened last year?"

Out of habit, Natalie pressed her hand on her chest. "My business partner and I took on way too much. I have a tendency of doing that." She bounced her eyebrows and smiled at him. He grinned and nodded with understanding. "It's my weakness, and my strength, I guess. When there is a challenge, or a job, I strive for excellence. I pour my heart and soul into it on behalf of my clients—" She stepped in closer to him and spoke from the corner of her mouth, "I get a little bossy, too."

Thad tipped his head back in a chuckle. "Bossy? You? Never."

Natalie lifted her shoulder to her cheek in a half shrug, half surrender to his sarcasm. "It's taken a lot to get where I'm at professionally. I can't help but channel all my energy and focus wherever it's needed."

He steadied his gaze on hers. "I get it. And especially after spending this season in Rapid Falls. Everyone is so connected. If you care so much for your clients, I'm not surprised you want the best for the retirement residents." His gaze wavered as he peered out the door's small window into the dark alley. He stepped closer to Natalie, which was a surprising move because there was hardly space between them. One more step and she'd have to tilt her head up to see him clearly. "I want you to know I care, too. Even if event planning isn't my thing. I don't want you to think I don't care about the well-being of those folks. It's my job for a reason."

"Oh, Thad, I never thought you didn't care—" Her conversation with Darcie slammed into her thoughts. "Sometimes I get so focused on fixing things, I project my insecurity on others...and I pull away." She reached out a hand to his arm. "Thad, I understand the importance of guarding your time. For your son. I have to guard my time for my—" Natalie inwardly groaned at the next word on her tongue, *health*. It seemed so weak and silly. She was thankful her blood pressure was stable now. But she didn't want to admit that, although she'd managed to climb past all her learning difficulties, she now had something else threatening to keep her just shy of her full potential.

Thad placed his hand on hers, and cocked his head again, but this time, with a touching look of concern. "You have to guard your time for what?"

"My health, Thad." She rolled her eyes. His hand stayed firmly on top of hers, and he searched her eyes for more explanation. "It sounds so silly. But my doctor said I've been pushing myself too much at work. This staycation is pretty much prescribed."

"Natalie, you should have said something. I wouldn't have been so adamant that you take the lead. Believe me, I know what it's like to get carried away with work—" Thad squeezed her fingers gently. "Why do you think I'm carving out this time with my son?"

"You're doing a great job, Thad. Believe me, Gigi and her friends rave about your parenting skills."

"That's nice. It took me a good long while to balance out work and family. I mean, everything I ever did was for that dream of taking care of a family. Work, then grad school, then a promotion. It's a struggle to keep everything in order...but your health? Miss Cooper, that is *the* top priority." His eyes widened. "I'm surprised by your grandmother's persistence when you are supposed to be taking a break."

"She doesn't know." Natalie slipped her hand from beneath his. Immediate regret ensued at the loss of his comforting gesture. "I haven't told anyone around here. Don't want to worry them—" Across the busy diner, she saw Sean and Elisa enter. They waved, and she waved back. Thad did the same.

Before they finished their conversation, Brody appeared, squirming past the people standing next to them. "I'm done."

"Did you write a good one?" Thad placed his hand on top of Brody's stocking cap.

Brody shrugged his shoulders quickly. "I just drew a picture. I hate writing."

Natalie was about to agree with Brody—writing had always been a struggle—but she didn't want to encourage the kid to dislike academics. "A wise lady once told me that the more you write, the easier it gets."

"Easier or funner?" Brody didn't crack a smile, although Natalie had to bite the inside of her cheek to stop from giggling.

She tried to match Brody's serious question with a serious answer. "I guess, easier and more fun?"

Thad laughed. "Try writing a grant for funding."

"Oh, are you still doing that?" Natalie began to lead the way back through the diner.

"Of course. I told you, I care for the retirement community, too."

She paused, but quickly continued to weave through the chairs and tables, saying hello to a few acquaintances. Although, she was just fine standing in the back of the place, focused on one of the newest faces in Rapid Falls, finding complete satisfaction in Thad MacDougall's attention.

Even though the night air nipped at Thad's nose after being in the toasty diner, he was warm on the inside. He un-

derstood Natalie more than she knew. When he was working late hours during Brody's infancy, and then in grad
school during his toddler and preschool days, the struggle
of work-life balance was overwhelming. He said a small
prayer for Natalie's health, glancing at her as she walked
on the other side of Brody.

"My favorite part of the Jingle is ahead," Natalie remarked joyfully.

The corner of Main and Third was blocked off. The
porch of the women's shelter was covered in hay bales, and
a dark blue backdrop with painted stars hung over the entrance. Sitting in perfect stillness were a man and woman
dressed as Joseph and Mary, kneeling in front of a manger.

"A live nativity," Natalie whispered as they joined the audience. A small band sat beneath heat lamps in the blocked-
off area of the street, and they began to play "We Three
Kings." Behind the band, an empty lot had transformed
into a temporary coral with camels, sheep and goats. The
animal caretakers dressed up like the wise men and shepherds. They supervised families feeding the animals.

"Dad, can I go?" Brody's excitement brimmed in his
big brown eyes.

"Sure." Thad followed his son to the animal area. A wise
man opened the gate for Brody to go inside.

Natalie stood next to Thad. "Isn't this neat?"

"Up close and personal, huh?" Thad watched Brody
feeding two sheep under the watch of a man dressed like
a shepherd. Brody laughed as the sheep ate heartily from
his palms. "He loves animals. I've been resisting getting a
pet. But maybe it will help him."

"Help him?" Natalie leaned on the fence, her elbow
brushing his.

"To help his anxiety. To get comfortable around me, just
like he is with his mom and stepdad."

"He seems pretty close to you, Thad. Do you think his anxiety is more school related?"

"Sure, school's in the mix. But what came first?" He worked his jaw and admitted one of his uncertainties. "Is school a sore spot because of the rocky start he had? Our divorce was being finalized while he was just starting out. I know how much the younger years shape a kid." Thad lost his own mom when he was six. Memories of that sadness haunted him at many low moments of his life. He turned toward Natalie and shoved his hand in his coat pocket. The temperature must be dropping. "I am just a few years ahead of you in work-life-balance struggles. But instead of my health being affected, my family was." He grimaced at the admission of such a dark time in his life. A time when Maxine said the harshest words—laced with truth, but far bitterer than any that had been thrown at him before. When she filed for divorce, Thad was thankful that she and Derek honored Thad and Brody's relationship. He shuddered to consider not having decent custody rights with his own son.

"And you moved here to be close to him?" Natalie asked. "At least, that's the word around the knitting club." A coy smile crossed her lips, and she began to blow into her gloved hands.

Thad nodded, resisting the urge to gather up her hands and help her stay warm. "I thought things were looking up, but Brody's struggling in school. I can't help but wonder if I had been consistently in his life—maybe he'd be more adjusted."

Natalie opened her mouth to say something, but the announcer spoke in a microphone near the band.

"Good evening, folks. Please join us in singing 'Silent Night' before Mary and Joseph retire for the night." A faint ripple of laughter went through the crowd, and the band began to play again.

Brody came up to Thad and wrapped his arms around Thad's waist while everyone sang. Mary picked up a doll wrapped in swaddling clothes, and Joseph escorted her between the band and the crowd, then into the animal area. More hay bales were set up in the center of the corral. Mary and Joseph sat on top, while the wise men and shepherds surrounded them.

This time, they stood at the front of the crowd, and Brody didn't need to be on Thad's shoulders. Melodic voices rose all around. A gust of wind made his eyes water, and gasps went through the crowd. The frigid air was nearly unbearable. Natalie squeezed in close to Brody, smiling up at Thad. Natalie was a soprano, an angelic voice that he couldn't help but focus on for the rest of the song.

Thad resisted wrapping his arm around the woman who'd made this night one of his best nights in Rapid Falls. His mind and heart were at odds. From the outside looking in, Natalie seemed to fit in nicely with him and his son, showing them the town, encouraging Brody to participate in the festivities. But really, Thad and Natalie were in two different seasons of life. Thad had reaped the consequences of his own colliding seasons—a professional career and life as a family man. There was no use considering anything more with a woman so motivated and successful as Natalie.

Thad swallowed on a lyric and released a stuttering sigh. A relationship was the last thing Thad MacDougall should be considering right now.

With relationships came expectations, and clearer than this wintry night sky, was the truth that he'd failed miserably to meet another's expectations in the past. A mistake he'd never make again.

Chapter Thirteen

Tuesday morning's silver sky was heavy with its promise of snow. Natalie buried her face in her scarf, while Lex tugged on the leash as they hurried into the retirement center.

After hanging up her coat, she joined the group of women in their typical spot. Susie, Tina, Marge and Gigi sat in the main living area, knitting and chatting.

"Good morning, all." Natalie squirmed past Gigi's armchair with a squeeze of her shoulder, then sat on the hearth, happy for the fire crackling and heating away. Lex received attention from each woman, then reclined at Natalie's feet with a bone.

"How are you doing this morning, Nattie?" Gigi peered over her glasses propped low on her nose. "You look tired."

"I do?" She felt great, a little chilled to the bone, but nothing a cozy fire and her travel mug filled with apple cider wouldn't fix. "I'm not tired at all."

"I think your grandmother is curious about your date last night." Tina crossed her legs and continued knitting as if she'd just mentioned the weather.

Natalie's gaze skittered around the group, landing on the usual suspects—Marge's tight dimple, Susie's raised eyebrow, Tina's pursed lips and Gigi's anticipatory stare. "If you all are talking about the Main Street Jingle, then you've been misinformed." Although the mention of last night rendered the fire behind her unnecessary. Heat unfurled inside her chest. She resisted placing her hands on her cheeks. Instead, she sipped from her mug, avoiding staring at anyone directly.

"Oh, sweet Natalie, don't you know?" Marge giggled. "We have spies all around." The women laughed while Natalie bit her cheeks to keep from smiling. "You may refuse to define your outing, but we all know better."

Gigi pressed forward. "I do hope you aren't too distracted by his good looks, though. The festival is drawing near."

"Gigi!" Natalie set her cup on the hearth next to her. "I was simply giving Thad *and* his son an insider scoop on the Jingle. And no, I wasn't distracted. In fact, we checked on auction items. Thad arranged to pick some up today. All is exactly as it should be."

"Yes, yes, it is." Tina bounced her eyebrows and shifted her gaze to Thad, who'd just entered the room. Laughter bubbled among the group.

Tina's twisted take on Natalie's words was in good knitting club form, Natalie must admit.

"Good morning, everyone." Thad spoke while he filled up his coffee mug at the coffee station. Natalie tried to manage her posture, her facial expression, anything that might spark Tina Delaney's knack for shaping the perfectly innocent feature into a rumor-worthy subject. But if that woman could read minds—oh, Natalie would be in trouble. Thad was exceptionally handsome this morning. It must be that sea green sweater complementing his brown eyes. His lively smile didn't help. No wonder the man was hired by the retirement community board. Most of these women were around that table. And Thad must have taken some course on charming each generation. Or at least Gigi's. *Charm* was hardly in Natalie's vocabulary, unless it had something to do with a dangly piece of silver on a napkin holder or a bridesmaid-gifted bracelet.

If Natalie had ever been *charmed* by a man—it was to her detriment. She'd nearly put her whole career on hold for a charmer. And now, while her career was on a temporary hold, she would not fall for the knitting club ploy—no matter how tempting.

But Thad barely looked at her this morning. Instead, he addressed Susie. "We have all the extra gingerbread supplies packed up and ready to be delivered to the women's shelter."

"Great, thanks, Thad. I am heading off to tutor around lunchtime. I'll drop them off then."

Now, Thad glanced over at Natalie. "I see that Lex is perfectly happy this morning."

"Yes, Brody had nothing to worry about. Lex didn't miss the Jingle one bit." She smiled a little too big, at least for the audience around them. She tried to ignore the smug expressions she could see from the corner of her eyes. Locking her gaze with Thad's was more comfortable than drawing any unnecessary attention.

"That's good. I am impressed with Rapid Falls, more and more." He glanced around the group.

Tina crossed her arms on top of her multicolored yarn. "What impresses you most?"

Natalie nearly rolled her eyes, but she thought better of it.

"The traditions, I guess." Thad stuck a hand in one pocket and sipped from his mug. Now more magazine model than retirement community director. "It helped having Natalie show us around Main Street last night. I think it left a great impression on Brody."

"Traditions have a way of grounding you to a place." Gigi sighed and smiled at Natalie.

"So do people," Marge added.

"Yes, they do." Tina obviously couldn't resist accentuating the point.

Hal Kerr entered from the nursing home wing. Hal walked ever so slowly—methodically and with great concentration on the effort of lifting up a foot, then his cane, then the next foot. Edward Shaw, the nurse practitioner, appeared behind him.

Thad skirted around the couch, toward the men. "Speaking of people, there is one of the most fascinating fishermen I've met since my own grandfather." Thad walked up to Hal and Edward, and they all took a seat at the table behind Gigi's armchair. Natalie overheard Thad say, "I tried to start a tourney this year for the festival, Hal. Maybe your seniority around this town would help convince the committee."

Natalie whipped her head to him, knowing fine well that by *committee*, he meant her. Thad was staring at her with intensity in the most adorable, playful way. He was teasing, wasn't he?

Her mind flipped through the probability of his fishing tournament idea doing anything but muddling the tradition of a festival within these walls. The festival was not going to extend out at a pond on the other side of town.

Hal muttered something that Natalie couldn't quite hear, and the ladies moved on to discussing Christmas plans with their families.

After a couple of games of cribbage, Natalie helped Susie take the gingerbread houses to the car.

"Piper Hudson is putting on a Christmas fair for the kids at the shelter. She said they have twelve under the age of eight years old."

"How are the Hudsons?"

"They're great. Piper and Lance live on an acreage just across from the orchard. Their baby boy, Donny, is a doll.

I've been helping their daughter, Maelyn, with some math tutoring."

"You are so good at that." Natalie set her box down in Susie's trunk.

"It really depends on the child. Some of the kids refuse to listen. Maelyn is very well-mannered. But I will try with anyone the principal refers to me."

Natalie wondered if the principal had mentioned Brody. She was about to ask but then thought better of it. First, she had no business prying just because she'd spent some time with the MacDougalls. And second, and most critical, Susie wasn't so far above the rest of her friends as to not take Natalie's interest in anything to do with Thad as interest in Thad himself. Although, sneaky giddiness taunted Natalie's plan to guard herself from any future relationship disaster at the very mention of Thad this morning.

And then seeing him across the room?

Natalie may as well just end her staycation now and move on to the next event. Her heart was wildly out of control, in the very best way. She couldn't risk rejection like she had with her ex. He'd caused her to spiral back into the self-doubt that had plagued her from middle school. What would happen now, if she asked for a new relationship this Christmas? There were no guarantees when it came to love, and she'd experienced the risks greatly outweighing the benefits at this point in her career.

As they crossed the parking lot again, she thought about her first night back. She'd nearly run into that sign because her inventory had distracted her from the back seat.

What disaster would occur if she was vulnerable in the romance department amid work pressure and taking care of her health? Nope, not worth taking the chance. She loved her life too much to add anything to her Christmas list.

* * *

Thad loved talking with Hal Kerr this morning. Fishing was a deep love instilled in him by Thad's grandfather. It was the one pastime Thad and his own father had in common—when his father wasn't on business trips and working all hours of the night.

Thad might not be one to organize an event—unless a whole town expected it—but he had the heart of a fisherman. The opportunity to gather other fishermen in the area and sit on the ice from dawn till noon? Sounded pretty divine. And he sensed Hal's enthusiasm. The man appeared teary-eyed talking about not having the chance to fish this year. His health was declining after he suffered a stroke last spring.

Even if a tourney day wouldn't work for the festival weekend, like Natalie absolutely made clear, maybe Thad could set aside some time in the new year and look into tentative dates.

He sighed and pressed back in his office chair. He certainly didn't need to add to his list of to-dos. After the holidays, he would be completely exhausted. And he wouldn't have Natalie around for impromptu advice.

He wondered if she would be interested in planning something outside of her comfort zone. He snickered at the thought of her initial reaction to his idea for a fundraiser. She'd looked at him as if his nose was glowing red.

The thought of working with her after the new year, however, initiated a ripple of hope in his chest. Having more time with Natalie, and watching her do what she loves? He'd caught a glimpse of her excitement with Sean and Elisa. He'd love to see her in action for something he loved, too—like a fishing tournament. Thad ran his hand over his hair and shook his head on a breathy laugh. That would be something he could manage to set aside time for.

He closed the festival binder on his desk and opened

up the grant application on his computer. He had to focus and stop thinking about Natalie. First, she had rejected his fishing tournament idea completely, and second, he'd never meet her expectations. Not that he knew what they might be, but his own experience was enough to keep him single for a good long while.

If he was honest with himself, the main reason for considering Natalie for the hypothetical job wasn't as much to do with a stellar fishing event, but a chance to be with the stellar event planner, with or without the event to plan.

That afternoon, Thad finished up some meetings with potential residents, then checked his email. Some of Natalie's contacts had replied to his email asking for donations.

Natalie would be excited. Maybe she was right about raising more funds. Especially when one of the donors offered a pricey package to a golf course, and another was offering a night in a bed-and-breakfast along the Mississippi River. Besides the packages, each donor mentioned purchasing entire tables for the dinner, and one donor said he was sending the save-the-date to his men's ministry group. They were talking about a date night with their wives and the renowned Christmas Festival seemed just the thing they'd enjoy.

Thad immediately pulled out his phone and texted Natalie, Your Christmas wish might just come true, Miss Cooper. Received some generous news from a couple of the contacts you gave me.

He added the specific details to a subsequent text, then waited for Natalie's response. His alarm went off to remind him to pick up auction baskets. Thad left the center and drove to Main Street. He picked up his phone to see if Natalie had responded. Nothing yet.

When Thad entered Sally's Boutique the door chime sang.

He wasn't sure if the woodsy, berry scent was from the many wreaths hanging on a shiplap wall, the large vases filled with dried plant material and tall candle votives, or if it was pumped into the room to entice customers to sit and stay a while. Thad was tempted to try out the pin-striped armchair displaying a casually tossed throw blanket and a pillow donning Joy to the World embroidered in a crimson thread.

Warm light from beaded chandeliers and ornamental lamps of various heights dotted the different displays on shelves, tables and on top of stacks of old books. Was it really winter outside? This place was an oasis of warmth.

Sally appeared, swinging aside a colorful curtain draped across an entryway behind the counter. "Oh, Thad, you are just in time." She held open the curtain and Natalie walked through carrying a crate. "We have the centerpieces nearly ready to go."

"Oh, I thought I was picking up the auction baskets."

"You are." Sally's sparkling gaze boomeranged between him and Natalie. "But for now, Natalie and I were talking about ordering from Sweet Lula's. It's about that time of day when a little chitchat and coffee are called for. You are just in time, isn't he, darling?" She wildly wagged eyebrows and nudged Natalie with her elbow.

Thad narrowed his eyes, suspicious the woman was signaling similar knitting club antics that Natalie had accused Marge of last night.

"Whatever, Sally." Natalie grunted and shuffled forward. "Could I get a little help here?"

"Oh sure." Thad hurried around the counter, noticing Sally stepping back—instead of forward—to help Natalie.

He lifted the crate, his hands brushing against Natalie's. "I've got it," he murmured, locked in her thankful gaze. Bluer than blue eyes shone above the cedar greenery and tapered candles in his arms.

"Thanks." Natalie pulled her hands away while Thad set the crate on the counter. "I was in the area, so I thought I'd check on these." She threaded her finger through a ribbon loop on one of the centerpieces. "Aren't they perfect?"

"Sure, perfect." But he was looking at her, wondering why she was checking in on festival logistics. However, he couldn't mention anything about her health with Sally standing there, watching them intently.

Natalie didn't seem the least bit stressed, so he shouldn't be too concerned about her involvement. In fact, she was completely enthralled with the decor literally at her fingertips. She spoke softly, "The only way to do great work is to love what you do." A whimsical smile crossed her lips and her gaze danced with Thad's. No, Natalie wasn't stressed out, she was inspired.

"Hey, didn't Steve Jobs say that?" Thad cocked his head. His mouth quirked with a questioning grin.

Natalie nodded and giggled. "Sally, your love for decor reminds me how much I love my job."

"But you aren't working for us," Thad reminded her, now feeling it necessary to keep that boundary for Natalie's health. "Even if you've pulled through in the past few days more than anyone has in the past month." She merely shrugged. Thad inquired, "I assume you haven't seen your texts?"

Natalie pulled her phone from her back pocket. "No, I haven't looked—" She read her text, then stared up at him on a gasp. "Are you serious?" Her eyes were bright with excitement. "Oh, Thad, this is amazing." Without hesitation, the woman flung her arms around his neck. "We might just have a chance at raising the funds."

"It's all you." Thad wanted to snake his arms around her waist and hold on for a while. But he caught the mischievous grin of Sally Grover and thought better of it. Thad patted Natalie quickly, and they pulled apart.

Natalie clapped her hands together. "Okay, we have got to be sure to live up to the event's obvious reputation. Centerpieces are done. Auction baskets?" Her brow arched in question as she glanced between Sally and Thad.

Thad affirmed, "That's why I am here. Picking them up today."

"Yes, yes. I will go finish getting them ready. Just need to wrap them with cellophane." Sally walked to the back room. "And add a beautiful bow, of course," she called out as the curtain swooshed close behind her.

"Great," Natalie replied over her shoulder, then faced Thad. "Now, our biggest crowd-pleaser is the pageant. You're certain that's all taken care of?"

"Natalie, it's all good," he assured and stepped closer. "You need to take it easy. I don't want you to get too worked up over the plans." Without a thought, he reached out and rubbed her arm.

She froze. Her gaze was questioning at first, but then she seemed to melt against his touch. "I forgot you knew, for a minute. Strange to have someone face-to-face, reminding me." She tilted her head and amusement activated her dimples. "I am not that fragile. This is exciting, Thad." She clutched his arm and bounced on her toes. "You don't realize how important these donors are—not just for the auction but by drumming up interest in the community. We might need more centerpieces." She seemed to inventory the crate, then started counting on her fingers how many more they might need. Her forehead crinkled upward as her hand flew to her mouth. "Sally's got work to do."

Thad laughed, completely entranced by this woman. "You are adorable—" Did he say that out loud? All the light in the room seemed to dance in her bright blue eyes.

Amused, flattered? Or maybe a little shocked herself? The muscles in his face went slack. "Um, I mean—" He was caught up in her enthusiasm, that's all. She *was* adorable. "Sorry, that was just—"

"Not true?" She scowled playfully.

"No, I…" He stepped back and rubbed his jaw. "Uh, I must admit, your excitement for the festival is adorable." He just shrugged his shoulders.

"Oh, okay. My *excitement* is adorable. Got it." She rolled her eyes and leaned on the counter, crossing her arms.

A current rolled in Thad's torso, and he stepped forward, placing his palm on the counter by her hip. His face was just a couple of inches from hers. "You know exactly what I mean, Miss Cooper." His gaze traveled along her smooth cheekbones, long lashes, rosy lips. "You are actually not adorable at all." Her eyes widened with utter shock, but just like he enjoyed watching her transform when she read his text, he'd savor this moment now, when he'd admit exactly what he meant by *adorable*. "You are beautiful, Natalie. Especially when you are doing what you love. I can't help but think it."

Her teeth grazed her bottom lip, and her lashes fluttered. "My, Thaddeus, you are too kind."

Thad jerked his head back. "*Thaddeus?* Was that a joke?"

Natalie's cheeks filled with color, and she nervously laughed. "Sorry, it just came out." She placed a hand on his coat lapel and glanced over her shoulder in the direction of Sally now chattering on the phone, it seemed. "Um, I think we should probably get these things loaded up, don't you?"

Thad's alarm went off on his phone. "Oh no, I need to pick up Brody from school." He hurried around the counter. "I haven't even finished gathering all the baskets."

Natalie's shoulders lifted as she breathed in deeply. "No problem, Thad. I've got you covered."

"I can't ask you to do that. It's my responsibility—"

"What? No, I am here and have nothing else going on. Go."

"Thank you, Natalie." He pulled his gloves from his pockets and hurried through the shop, spun around and took the last few steps backward. "If you have any trouble, just text. I can always swing by tomorrow." She gave a thumbs-up.

Thad raced to his truck. Only when he pulled into the school pickup line did the effects of his afternoon hit him at full force.

What had just happened between him and Natalie?

Thad said a quick prayer, thankful that losing track of time hadn't made him so late that Brody was the only kid waiting.

Brody ran up to the truck and yanked open the back door. "Hey, Dad, there's a light tour tonight."

"What?" Thad slung his arm on the seat, looking over his shoulder at his son.

"Yeah, it's on Boxwood and Birch. That's what my friend said. The first twenty cars get a cool bag of goodies at the end of the neighborhood." Brody tossed his backpack on the seat next to him and buckled up. "Can we go?"

"Of course. It's Christmastime, isn't it?"

"Yippee," Brody declared. He looked down at an orange slip in his hand. His expression went from glee to anxiety in a split second. He shoved the paper in his pocket.

The car behind Thad honked, and he realized he was holding up the line. He shifted the truck in gear and drove out of the school parking lot, trying to decide if he wanted to ask Brody about the slip. Thad was overcome with the joy of seeing his little boy excited.

Why would he risk ruining that right now?

Chapter Fourteen

The sun broke through the clouds, betraying the promise of snow. Even though the temperature was barely in the double digits, the wind had died down, making for a decent afternoon. Natalie unloaded the silent auction items and set them on her dining room table. She could have dropped them off at the retirement center, but she wanted to check on Lex.

While she watched the dog kick up snow in the backyard, a familiar impending doom sat in her chest. What if the festival disappointed those new donors and their friends? Could the Rapid Falls Retirement Community Festival live up to the reputation of years past with Thad in charge? Not that the man wasn't reliable. He pulled off a fun choir concert and gingerbread house event for preschoolers. And he was a devoted father to his son. Thad was one of the good guys…and his simple compliment today had sent her pulse racing into the more-than-friends zone.

She opened the door for Lex, gave her a treat, then glanced over the auction baskets once more. Lindsey called while Natalie was arranging the cellophane so it wouldn't crease.

"Hey, Lindsey, how's it going?"

"We're good. My brother and his wife are back from

their getaway. I finally have some time to myself. What's that crinkling sound?"

"Oh, I'm just arranging some gift baskets for the festival."

"Sounds like you are resting hard on your staycation."

"Don't worry, I am. I offered to pick them up since Thad had other things come up. Besides, I wanted to be sure the additional items I acquired were included."

"And?"

"They were." Natalie sighed. "I just hope everything else falls into place."

Lindsey cleared her throat dramatically. "Not yours to do, friend."

"I know, I know. This has been a great staycation so far. You should have seen me last night. We strolled along every square foot of Main Street and didn't talk about the festival one bit."

"Ah, so Gigi's out and about after her hip issues? That's great."

"Gigi— Oh, no. I went with Thad and Brody."

"The director? Hmm, are you sure you aren't secretly planning?" Lindsey should have been a detective instead of business manager.

"Yes, Linds. I ran into them and showed them around. A perfectly non-shoptalk shop walk." She laughed.

"Ha ha. I am curious what this guy looks like. You've been spending an awful lot of time with him. Or maybe not so awful?" Forget detective, maybe honorary knitting club member was more like it.

"He's…okay. Handsome. And nice. I actually told him about my blood pressure."

"It sounds like you two are getting close."

"We just keep finding ourselves in the same place at the same time."

"I see. Sounds like you're hardly resting on your staycation." Lindsey's suspicious tone sent Natalie's eyes rolling. "Well, take care of yourself and make sure those baskets don't keep you up at night. I'm going to go take a bubble bath."

"You are the best auntie ever and totally deserve it."

After they said their goodbyes, Natalie was a little uneasy about all that Lindsey seemed to pick up from their conversation. Natalie shouldn't consider Lindsey echoing what Gigi's friends had implied. Natalie's heart was bruised beyond repair after her last relationship. She couldn't allow a fuzzy feeling to risk sabotaging her potential. She needed some fresh air.

This time of year, Natalie never let an Iowa-warmish day go by without taking advantage of her walking shoes, even for short, chilling bursts. So, she bundled up, unraveled the new leash she'd bought after their last escapade and took Lex for a walk before dinner.

Many neighbors were outside adding Christmas decor to their yards. Lex wouldn't let her slow down to chat with anyone, but she gave a friendly wave to the Smithsons on their left and Mr. Bower across the street.

She gripped the leash tighter as they approached the park. "Not today, missy." Her words formed a cloud in the crisp air. If only Lex spoke English. She started to whine and pull toward the play equipment roped off until the great melt sometime in March. "Absolutely not." Natalie tried to veer the dog to the left. Slipping and sliding on the pond without Thad to help her out was not a risk she was willing to take. "No, Lex." She shortened the leash with another wrap around her glove. But Lex's whole body shook with excitement, and she yelped, her stare fixed on the dormant play area.

"Okay, we'll just go back instead of continuing around

the block." She reprimanded in the same tone her mom would use whenever Natalie had refused to do her chores. But a movement by the slide caught her eye and evoked a deep bark from Lex. Natalie squinted. Yep, a kid was sitting on the bottom of the slide. She scanned the rest of the area for an adult.

Nobody else was in sight. The sun was quickly sinking behind the spidery branches of Saint George's churchyard in the distance. The child just sat there.

"Okay, Lex. Let's check it out. We don't want the little guy getting stuck outside when the sun's gone down." She shivered as she considered the deadly overnight temps being a very real threat during an Iowa winter.

Natalie jogged beside the eager Lex, winding down the shoveled sidewalk instead of tromping through the snow like last time. She carefully took the snow-covered steps down to the playscape. The boy was wearing a familiar cap with earflaps.

"Brody, is that you?"

Brody stood up and wiped his nose with his sleeve. His face was red and blotchy, and he didn't look at Natalie directly. Just Lex. Lex jumped and tugged. Natalie unwound the leash but made sure to keep her grip while the dog pulled her to Brody.

"Where's your dad?" Natalie asked as he crouched down and hugged Lex.

"At home."

"Does he know you are here?"

Brody shook his head. "I don't want to talk to him."

"Brody, he's probably worried about you. I have to let him know you are safe."

The boy's shoulders slumped, and he kept his full attention to the dog.

Natalie texted Thad, I found Brody on the playground at the park. Want to meet at my house to get him?

Thad responded right away. I'm leaving now.

Natalie didn't want to tell Thad that Brody didn't want to talk to him. He can hang out with Lex and me for a bit.

No, I am coming.

Meet me in my driveway then.

Ok.

"Brody, let's head to my house. Your dad is meeting us there."

"I said, I don't want to talk to him."

"I know. But you can't stay here all night. It's going to get cold really fast." Natalie was starting to shiver.

Brody huffed and stood again. He kept his chin down and walked alongside Lex as they headed home.

"Care to talk about it?"

"I am just a loser."

Natalie's mouth dropped. "Brody! Don't say that."

"That's what a girl said at school." Brody scowled. "I didn't finish my test. Everyone else finished, though. The girl said I was a loser."

"Kids can be mean, huh?" Natalie had plenty of school-age experiences shoved beneath all her grown-up success. "But she obviously doesn't know you."

Brody looked over at her. "But I got an orange slip. That's not good. I didn't want to show Dad. He'll just think I am a loser, too. But he saw it." His eyes bubbled. "Now, Dad's going to take away Christmas." He crossed his arms over his thick winter coat.

Natalie swallowed a startled laugh. "That's not true.

After cutting down your tree, eating in an igloo and going to the Jingle, I think he's pretty committed to making Christmas a go." She reached over and playfully tapped him with her fist.

Brody didn't say anything. Natalie followed his gaze. Thad's truck pulled into her driveway. The slam of his door echoed in the still winter air, and he took long quick strides toward them, meeting them on the sidewalk by her mailbox. Natalie allowed Lex to sniff around the patch of snow, uncertain if she should invite them inside, especially since Thad's blanched face and steel-eyed gaze hinted that he was not up for hospitality. It was getting colder in more ways than one.

"Brody, you scared me." Thad stood across from him. "I thought you were in your room finishing your test."

"I don't see why I have to work on it when I worked all day." Brody kicked the brick of the mailbox structure.

"So, you leave without telling me?"

"You said I can't see the Christmas lights unless I finished. Well, the test is way too hard, so I decided to come see them for myself."

Thad cast a look of exasperation in Natalie's direction.

"Brody, you can't sit out here. It's not safe in these temperatures," Natalie chimed in. "The lights will be up all season, even after you finish your test."

"Not the Tour of Lights, though. My friends were talking about the synchronized lights on the corner and the goodies for the first cars." Brody hooked his gloved hand on his father's arm. "Please can I finish the test after the lights?"

"Oh no—" Natalie groaned. "The tour!" She spun around and stared at her naked roofline and light-less shrubs. "I forgot to put up the lights." The tour was a Rapid Falls tradition. Cars would wait in line all night to drive down her street, and tonight was the kickoff. She couldn't be the only house without lights. Her father would be so disappointed.

Thad looked at his watch. "It's almost five o'clock. What time does the tour start?"

"Seven. Two hours. How can I do all that in two hours?" Natalie couldn't believe she wasn't prepared for this tradition.

"We can help." Thad eyed the roofline of the first story, the porch column and the shrubs along the front of the house. "The light clips are up along the roof already. Might not be the brightest house on the block, but we can make it decent." He raised an eyebrow at Brody. "As long as Brody promises to work on his test when we get home."

"I will, I promise." Brody's face lit up. He'd rather do manual labor than schoolwork. If Natalie wasn't so frustrated with herself, she'd laugh. But this was no laughing matter. The Cooper house very nearly became the black hole on the street.

Could they really get the lights up in time?

Natalie opened the garage, while Thad tried to calm down his emotions. Had he come down too hard on Brody? Once they got home from school, Thad had to ask about that orange slip Brody seemed to hide.

It needed Thad's signature to say that Brody would finish the test at home without any help. Thad was upset that Brody hadn't been up-front about it. He'd never had to discipline Brody for character mistakes. But he didn't want to slack on his responsibility as a parent. Taking away a fun outing tonight seemed a natural consequence for unfinished schoolwork. But then the kid left the house without telling him. And Brody's excitement from earlier haunted him the rest of the afternoon.

Doing the right thing seemed to cost a whole lot of peace.

Now, while Natalie handed Brody the light-up candy canes to attach to the porch rail, Brody was perfectly happy. Smiling even. From a distance, Thad unraveled the lights for the roof, he prayed for wisdom in this situation.

"Here you go, Thad." Natalie set up the ladder at the corner of the garage. "I'm glad we only have a one-story house, aren't you?" Her face was bright with enthusiasm. "And I am so thankful you are helping me." She squeezed his arm as she passed by. "I don't know what I would have done without you."

And although Thad was not so certain he'd make Father of the Year, he was happy to be the one person Natalie could count on right now. And that was nearly as confusing as keeping on top of his son's schoolwork.

After about an hour of focused work, Thad and Brody headed to the end of the driveway while Natalie waited on the porch to turn on the outlet strip.

"Son, you did a great job with the porch. Those candy canes are in perfect alignment with each rail."

"Thanks, Dad. I can't wait to see it. It's going to be awesome."

Brody's fingers were threaded together, and his brow pushed up his fur-lined cap in eager anticipation. No anxiety, no uncertainty in his voice. Thad bristled at the next task—

Brody finishing the test before school tomorrow. Surely now, his son would have the drive to do his work without complaint.

The house lit up with hundreds of lights in three different waves. First, the roof lined in red and white bulbs that also wrapped around the two porch columns. Second, the candy canes glowed, lining the stairs and along the front of the porch. The wreath on the front door sparkled with twinkle lights. Third, the bushes beneath the porch railing and the tree trunks of the two trees in the yard shone bright with an onslaught of twinkle lights, too.

"Hooray!" Brody yelled with a fist in the air.

Thad chuckled. Natalie hurried down the porch steps and ran toward them. Thad instinctively held out his arm. She joined him, wrapping her arm around his waist. Warmth spread through him. They stood and admired the lights together, in a casual side embrace, with his son standing just in front of them.

"Thank you so much," Natalie half whispered, and pulled in closer to him. "It's perfect."

He shouldn't hold on so firmly to this woman, but her unfaltering embrace and sincere gratitude enticed Thad to believe he was doing something right—even if it had nothing to do with his parenting skills. Offering to help Natalie was a natural response to a friend in trouble, even if it were for a simple neighborhood tradition. He'd never been able to stand by and watch someone struggle without giving a helping hand. Thad considered that one of his better qualities. Come to think of it, during his most stressful weeks of working and studying, hadn't he adjusted his priorities to help his wife with their son? At least, he'd like to remember it like that. Even if his gut still twisted with the guilt of not being fully present those days.

Natalie patted Brody's hat. "How about a hot chocolate to go? It's always nice to have something sweet while you study."

"Ugh." Brody groaned and turned around, pushing his head back as he stared up at Thad. "Do I have to finish the test? I hate word problems."

Natalie's gaze searched Thad's face as if she had something to say but contemplating the best way to express it. She slowly pulled away. "Maybe the cocoa will inspire you, Brody. And if there is one piece of advice I can give—

take your time. Nobody will know how long it took you. That's the home court advantage." She winked at his son, then offered Thad undivided attention with a twinkle in her blue eyes.

They followed her through the garage and into the kitchen. While she made up two to-go cups, Thad wrestled with the looming battle of getting Brody to do his homework, the guilt for taking so long to move to the same town as his son, and the wonder at having lived in this town all these months and only now getting to know Natalie.

What was life like before this woman became a constant companion during this most wonderful time of year?

Chapter Fifteen

That evening, Natalie sat at the window of the dining room, her lap covered in her favorite throw blanket, and Lex sitting with her back pressed against Natalie's legs. The radio was flipped to the station playing the synchronized light show around the corner. She enjoyed watching the lights outside the window, even if they were mostly headlights and taillights crawling between her simply lit abode and the multicolored extravaganza across the street.

Mostly, Natalie's mind kept rolling back to the best part of this tour—her personal sneak peek at the lights in the arms of Thad MacDougall. All right, she wasn't exactly in his arms, but he had his arm wrapped around her shoulders. It had been so firm and secure, as if he was the anchor that kept her in place on this wintry night. Maybe it wasn't just his arm, but the cozy warmth, the familiar cadence of his voice and the irresistible cedarwood scent that was quickly becoming her favorite aroma of the season.

What was she thinking? This was not the time to cave to the knitting club's—and Lindsey's—implications. If Natalie thought the fall was busy, the spring would be even more so. She couldn't think about anything romantic here in Rapid Falls when she would soon be whisked away living her own dream by dream-making for five brides, a couple of fundraisers and an Easter extravaganza for a corporate farmer.

However, while she was staycationing, she couldn't ignore the fact that a friendship had blossomed with Thad.

She pulled out her phone, curious if Thad's bargaining skills with Brody had worked.

How is Brody's test coming along?

He's working on it now. But I can't tell if he's just staring at the page, or really reading the problems. He may be thinking of Christmas lights, and we would never know.

Natalie's mouth quirked at his humor. Stand your ground, Dad. He's blessed to have such an attentive parent.

Natalie thought about her parents back when she was in school. They had done whatever they could to help her stay on top of her work. When Mom had set up the tutoring session with Susie, Natalie reacted nearly the same as Brody had today—although Natalie hadn't run off. Instead, she stomped to her room and slammed the door. Her greatest fear was having kids see her with a tutor. Getting one-on-one help in school? That was a social no-no among preteens.

Over the next half hour, Natalie checked her phone to see if Thad had responded, but he never did. The auction baskets began to irritate her, sitting on her table instead of in the retirement center. What else needed to get done that was on hold? She began to flip through the lists sitting on the rolltop desk. Her phone rang from the dining room. Her stomach did a little flip, and she raced across the house. She ignored the sinking feeling when she saw Gigi's name on the screen.

"Hi, Gigi."

"Hello, dear. I am beside myself." Her grandmother's voice was shaky. "The youth group theater director, Carrie, was here for dinner and said that they were short on kids for the pageant. And even worse, the little girl who was narrating is now going on vacation over Christmas, so there's a huge hole in the cast. I am so worried that this festival is going to be a flop. We can't have it without a pageant, Natalie."

"What can I do?" Natalie's question was the first one to usually come out of her mouth in face of impending disaster. And while it wouldn't stop the festival from happening, the pageant was listed as entertainment on the save-the-dates. Natalie's face heated just thinking about the unprofessionalism of not offering what was promised.

"I told Carrie that you would stop by first thing in the morning. You are the most reliable person in this town, Nattie. I am so glad you are home for Christmas."

"Gigi, don't you worry. I'll help figure it out. Get some rest," Natalie said sweetly, but she was starting to feel the weight of this event as if she'd planned the whole thing from the start.

The next day, after chatting with Carrie, Natalie left the community theater and went straight to the elementary school during dismissal. The halls were crowded with waist-high students.

The vice principal waited for her in the office. "You must be Natalie. I am Sharie Brown."

"Thank you for meeting me on such short notice." Natalie handed her the promised script.

She flipped through it. "Well, I am a huge fan of the Christmas Festival. I sat down with some of our teachers at lunch today. It sounds like we have a few kids who might enjoy participating."

"Great. Anything else I need to do?"

"No, I will get in touch with you once we get permission from their parents. Hopefully by the Friday when the first dress rehearsal is scheduled. And you are sure there is no memorization needed?"

"Yes. We need some animals and a narrator. The narrator can use the script."

Natalie returned to her car, elated that the vice principal was so willing to set things in motion, too. This festival was certainly loved by everyone in Rapid Falls. She headed to the retirement community to share the good news with Gigi.

By the time she hung up her coat in the cloakroom, then walked through the living area to the residents' hall, trying to ignore the wear and tear on the old Christmas decorations, an idea formed in her mind that would qualify as knitting club sneakiness in the greatest degree. But it had nothing to do with romance and everything to do with regretting she ever told Thad about her blood pressure.

Natalie needed to take charge of the festival's final details, and especially the pageant. If it was anything less than perfect, she worried about disappointing not only the town but also the folks who were driving from other communities in wintry weather and trusting the event enough to give pricey auction items.

Natalie needed to be there, overseeing all of it. A few days ago, the whole town would have cheered her on. But she had to go and spill her situation to Thad. His concern nearly melted her in a puddle on the boutique floor. She was certain he would stop her from taking charge.

But Natalie was fine. She hadn't had one episode this whole time. Even when she had missed her medicine.

After settling down at Gigi's kitchen table with a cup of tea, Natalie flipped through one of Tina's magazines that she'd loan out to Gigi when she was finished. "Gigi, when do you and the ladies meet again?"

"Well, the women who don't live here come every Thursday morning."

"Perfect timing to gather the supplies for a workday." Natalie nonchalantly turned the page, barely looking up. "Remember when Aunt Irene put everyone to work before the festival?"

"I haven't heard that we are doing that, dear."

"That never stopped you before." Natalie smiled. "Oh, and you all could work while the pageant rehearses. Perfect accompaniment, don't you think?"

"They'll rehearse tomorrow?"

"No, on Friday." Natalie scrunched her nose. She shrugged. "Would be fun to see a Christmas workshop come to life this year. I would make it a point to stop by, too."

She felt sneaky planting the idea in her grandmother's head. But the twenty-third was creeping closer, and the pageant was a big unknown at this point. Working on the complimentary gift bags for the dinner attendees and organizing the children's crafts for Klaus's Kiddie Korner would be such a festive time, especially listening to the pageant rehearsal in the next-door chapel room.

"What a fabulous thought, Natalie." Gigi clapped her hands.

"Gigi, you would be the perfect one to spearhead that operation."

"It will be a relief to know we are making progress. Thank you for thinking of it."

And as long as thinking it up was all her part seemed to be, Thad wouldn't be anxious about her exertion. "I love to brainstorm."

"And you have an excellent brain to do so." Gigi winked and sipped her tea.

After they finished chatting, Gigi decided to take a nap before dinner. Natalie headed to the storage closet by the conference room. It was locked. She would have to ask

Susie to take inventory of the materials for the kids' crafts. If not, Natalie could run to Waterloo's craft store on Thursday to stock up. She sent Susie a text as she walked back to get her things from the cloakroom. Her nerves were all frizzy—if that was even a condition nerves might find themselves in. It was more of a desire for instant knowledge about what was in the storage room closet than it was about her stress level. But even a little frizzy would have Lindsey greatly disapproving.

When she turned the corner, she nearly bumped into Brody, who was shaking off his winter coat in the middle of the lobby.

"Hi, Brody. Need some help with that?" Natalie caught a sleeve flying above his head.

"I got it."

"Hey, just the person I wanted to talk to." Thad appeared from the cloakroom. "Want to join us for some cookies?"

"Sure." She could use some chocolate. "Brody, I hope you got your test all finished."

Brody just shrugged and walked ahead to the complimentary cookies on the console table behind the couch. The living room was quiet this time of day. Only a couple of men sat in the far corner playing chess.

After getting their cookies, they sat down at the table behind Gigi's usual armchair.

Natalie bit into a double chocolate chunk cookie. "This is what the doctor ordered."

"Doctor?" Brody's quizzical look made her laugh. "I want to go to your doctor." A rare toothy smile formed on his face.

Thad appeared amused. "I got a call today, from the vice principal. Supposedly the pageant is in need of more students." He wiped the corners of his mouth with his napkin "And *you* are recruiting."

Natalie swallowed the chocolaty goodness of her next bite. "Yeah, Gigi called last night."

"You should have told me." He lowered his voice, "I don't want you to take on anything extra."

Natalie warmed at his thoughtfulness, glancing at Brody, who didn't seem to notice his father's compassion. "It was no problem, really." She would not mention the state of her nerves, or the workshop she just brainstormed with Gigi.

"Okay. Well, I think this is a great chance for Brody to get involved. His teacher sent an email to his class asking for help."

"What?" Brody was about to take another bite of his chocolate candy cookie.

"Brody, the pageant needs a narrator. I think you'd be a great fit." Thad's voice dripped with enthusiasm. "You are great when we play with the train. Your conductor voice would be perfect."

"No way." Brody set his unfinished cookie on his napkin.

"You don't have to memorize anything," Thad assured. "Just read a script."

"I don't want to do that. I can be a donkey. Like Natalie."

Natalie smiled. "You'd be pretty cute as a donkey."

Thad's grin became tight. He flicked a gaze at her and then back to his son. She didn't mean to step on toes, but apparently, she had.

Thad continued, "I think it would impress your teacher if you took a speaking role like this. Especially since she wants you to speak up in class more."

"No, I don't want to." Brody pushed his chair back. "Just leave me alone." He left the table and retreated to the far side of the room near the Christmas tree where some kids' toys sat in a basket.

Thad's smile faded. He picked at the corner of his napkin and let out a long sigh.

"Hey, you tried. But it might not be his cup of tea." Natalie spoke quietly, even though Brody was out of earshot. Besides, instrumental music played in a speaker above their table and another one was mounted just above the star of the Christmas tree where Brody sat. He couldn't hear the conversation.

"Ever feel like everything you planned for slipped away without even knowing it?" Thad grimaced.

Confusion dissolved any of the happy side effects of Natalie's chocolaty treat. "I didn't realize you had such high hopes for Brody's narrating career."

"No, not that." He ran his fingers over his short hair and hooked his hands on the back of his neck. "It just seems like everything is such a struggle now. Ten years ago, I would have told you I'd have a perfect family life. I thought, oh, I'd do things better than my own father. He was hardly around." He guffawed. "But I ended up following in my dad's footsteps for a while with my own son." Turmoil creased the corners of his eyes. "I never met Maxine's expectations. But I also never lived up to my expectations for myself."

"Thad, you are an amazing dad. Give yourself some credit."

He released a shaky breath and dropped his hands to the table. "I never thought I would be here, sharing custody with my ex-wife and her husband. They are great, and I am able to spend time with Brody now. But sometimes, I feel like I lost something that I never had to begin with. That ideal of being the perfect little family right about now. Yep, never had it. Not sure if I ever will. But this is certainly not what I expected my life to be like."

Natalie reached her hand across the table as a gesture of

empathy. "Sometimes we find ourselves listening to lies about what is good for us." Natalie had persuaded herself to think life with her ex was better than a career. She'd downsized her own dreams to fit into his. "But even if we veer off course for a while, God finds a way to nudge us to an even better plan. We've just got to listen." She threaded her fingers through his, hoping to convince this man that he was too hard on himself. "Thad, I don't know about your past, but I do know that you are far better at this parenting stuff than you think."

Thad squeezed her fingers and placed his other hand on top of hers. "I appreciate that, Natalie, I really do." He looked over at Brody. "I just don't know how to help him. His teacher says he's withdrawn, not wanting to participate. She suggested this might be a good opportunity for him."

Brody was playing with an old-fashioned Etch A Sketch. Natalie asked, "Did he do okay with the take-home test? I hadn't heard back from you."

Thad huffed. "Took him way longer than it should have. He's a daydreamer."

"Maybe he needs some extra help?"

"I wasn't supposed to help him."

"No, I mean in school. Daydreaming can be a sign of learning issues. It was for me. I got lost in my thoughts because the material was too complicated. Didn't keep my attention. You know, Susie's still tutoring. One-on-one is sometimes the best way."

Thad shook his head and his eyes dimmed—a look that flung her back to the stigma of a diagnosis. "This seems deeper than academics. He's only now stopped resisting going with me when it's my turn to pick him up. He just needs to know he's got a stable home life."

"What about his reading? You've proven his home life

isn't what's stopping him from keeping up with his reading assignments."

Thad's nostrils flared and he spoke curtly, "What kid loves to read at his age? This is something more than that." He sighed, pulled his hand away and stood. "Exactly why I moved here. To give him some consistency so he can focus on other things like school. Guess it's just taking time."

"Sure, but Thad—" She frowned. Should she really say what needed to be said? Was this any of her business? This man and his son had become regulars during her staycation. And Thad had obviously cared about protecting her health. Natalie really did care about helping him, too. She continued, "There are red flags with Brody's situation. Believe me, I know. Reading and test-taking were problematic for me. If you don't reach out to Susie, maybe he should get tested."

"Tested? For what?"

Natalie shrugged her shoulders. "A learning disability. Like dyslexia."

Thad's face reddened and he rolled his eyes. "Well, I guess that doesn't surprise me coming from you."

"What does that mean?"

"You are pretty adamant when you set your mind to something." His smile didn't reach his eyes.

"This isn't about me, it's about Brody." The defense in Thad's features was as strong as steel. "I didn't mean to offend you, but I know how hard it is to see what a kid needs sometimes. My parents weren't aware of my struggle at all in elementary school. And honestly, once I was diagnosed, it wasn't easy on them, either."

Thad's shoulders lurched on a sharp intake of air. "I am not worried about *diagnosing* him. You aren't listening at all." Was his lip quivering? He seemed upset.

Natalie sprung from her seat, all the frizzy nerves going

straight to her tingling elbows and shaky torso. Her defensiveness was rising. She despised being misunderstood. "Thad, I was listening. I just think you might be zooming right past some red flags."

Thad let out a bitter laugh. "You've been great giving your two cents about the festival, the food, the pageant. You really know your stuff." He shook his head and stepped back. "But please, don't tell me how to parent my kid. I am doing what I can. I don't need one more person in my life reminding me that I'm failing at this."

"I didn't say that—"

But Thad wasn't listening. He rounded the armchair and crossed the room, sitting on a stool next to his son. Brody's attention was on the toy in his lap. Natalie blinked back tears. A dull pang tightened her chest. Ugh. She balled up her napkin and decided it was time to go home.

The magnetic gray lines jerked up and down on the screen as Brody fiddled with the Etch A Sketch dials. Thad felt as though it matched his racing heart. As soon as he walked away from Natalie, that old guilt he'd wrestled with all these years for not meeting Maxine's expectations seemed far less worrisome than this sprig of shame for losing his temper.

But Natalie had crossed a line. He'd seen her toe the edge of a line with Darcie in the igloo—pushing her point emphatically. But then, Thad was impressed with her drive to do things right.

He'd thought her tenacity in the name of a longstanding tradition was admirable—and even fruitful now that they were growing a substantial guest list.

But talking about red flags with Brody when she'd only known them for a couple weeks was unacceptable.

He didn't need another person in his life scrutinizing how he should parent his son.

He patted Brody's shoulder. "If you want to be a donkey, that's okay with me."

"Really?" Brody kept turning the knob even though he was looking up at Thad.

"Sure. I was pushing you based on what I wanted." Those pesky expectations continually got the best of him. "That's not fair."

"No, it's not, I guess." Brody shook the toy and cleared all his doodles away. "Dad? Do you think I am a loser?"

"What?"

"I'm just not good at school." He rubbed his eye, and his bottom pushed lip out. "If it were a race, I'd lose." He placed the toy in the basket and gruffly crossed his arms in his lap.

"It's not a race, son. You are a winner no matter what." Brody had been Thad's greatest assurance that God was a loving Father. Something he had come to believe despite the insecurity of not knowing where he stood with his own father. "There has never been an instance in your nine years that I've thought of you as anything less. Do you hear me?"

Brody's chin quivered and he just stared at the floor, scowling. "You've got to think that. You're my dad. You love me no matter what."

Thad leaned his elbow on his knee and pressed his fist to his cheek, staring in half-belief. "Do you really think that?" Brody nodded, then slung an arm on Thad's thigh and rested his head. A rush of emotion exploded in Thad's chest, pricking at his eyes. He ran a shaky hand over Brody's golden hair.

For so long, Thad had assumed his son felt like Thad was more of an acquaintance; a distant relative who only stopped by at his convenience. Maybe it was because of all the accusations thrust in anger during his divorce. But he was more certain it had to do with Thad's own feelings toward his ever-traveling father. And then when Maxine remarried, Thad felt the need to fight harder for space in Brody's life. Only for a short period because Derek was very up-front about not replacing Thad, for which he was grateful.

Now, Brody was here, practically spelling out his own security in Thad's love. Whatever unmet expectations caused Thad to strive all these years didn't seem nearly as important as his son's loving gesture. Brody proved what was most important—Thad was secure in this relationship. How juvenile for a father to worry about such a thing. But Thad knew that's what this was all about. Security.

Brody sat up again. "Should we ask Natalie if she has those donkey ears from her picture? Those were cool."

Thad chuckled and rubbed Brody's back. "Maybe. I need to get some work done. Are you going to stay out here, or come hang in my office?"

"I'll stay here." His countenance fell as he picked at the cuff of his sleeve. "But can I wait to do homework at home?"

"You have homework?"

"Yes." Brody slumped and pushed his head back nearly between his shoulder blades in utter distress. Thad swiveled around. Natalie wasn't sitting at the table anymore. Of course. From the corner of his eye he saw the front door closed shut. She was gone.

He winced as he considered how much of his story he'd shared with her. And why was that? Why did he feel so comfortable with the staycationing event planner? Because Natalie was also toeing the edge of his dormant hope that something—someone—was out there who might be worth risking a second chance on…

Thad breathed in a stuttered breath. No, he was not reliable in the relationship arena. And besides, Rapid Falls was where he needed to be for Brody. Anything more than a cordial acquaintanceship with the golden child of the knitting club could bring a whole bunch of distress to all the connections he'd made in this town if it went awry. And with Thad's history, that would surely happen.

Chapter Sixteen

Their conversation replayed in Natalie's mind on the drive home. How had it spiraled out of control? She was trying to help. A sour feeling turned her stomach. If there was one flaw that Natalie would like to carve out of her ever-thinking brain, it was her need to give her two cents whenever she thought it was needed. Why did Natalie's opinion always need to be spoken out loud?

For advice-seeking brides, speaking her two cents was invaluable. But for budding new chefs, hurt by Natalie's need to prove herself, and single dads trying to work out a healthy relationship with their sons? Wow, Natalie should lean more heavily in the quiet part of the peace and quiet needed this December.

Lex greeted her in the mudroom. She pulled off her gloves and remembered the tender touch of Thad's hands encompassing hers. She hadn't hesitated to reach out and offer him comfort today. For the first time in a long while, Natalie was fine putting a pin in all the planning and details to give her full attention to a guy sitting across from her.

Maybe she was getting too close to Thad MacDougall. The guy had moved to Rapid Falls to be a better father to his son. Natalie was nowhere near the settle-down-for-family mode. Isn't that exactly what her ex had wanted for their future? More like the here and now, minus her business plans. Not that Natalie didn't want a family someday. And she had told him that. But he was not willing to give her the space to grow, too.

Lex spun in a circle and barked, wanting to play. She bent down and gave her some love. A reminiscent smile grew on Natalie's lips. Brody MacDougall had given her a glimpse at the joy of pouring your hard work and love into a child, even if it was just to support him in his reading and offer doggy playtime.

But she'd crossed a line discussing parenting tips with Thad. Of course she had. Did she really know what she was talking about? She knew the sneaky business of figuring out a learning disability, and Thad didn't seem to want to consider that for his son. An old feeling of inadequacy tugged at Natalie's heart. On top of her dyslexia, she had this pesky blood pressure problem.

Natalie Cooper was nowhere near being the person to speak about Thad's life. Of course, a father would want to resist the idea of a learning disability. A battle like that had left Natalie's esteem with scars—scars that grew her fighting persistence, but scars just the same.

Natalie owed Thad an apology for psychoanalyzing a purely parental situation. She was not a parent. And her own experience was not everyone's experience. A recent lesson, when Darcie shared her own perspective.

"Want to go outside, Lex?" Natalie flipped on the kitchen light and went over to the back door. The sun was low. She could make out its orange stain on the gray winter sky beyond the row of cedars marking the property line. Brody's snow people hadn't changed at all. No melting or added snow yet.

They were her only audience and Lex's stationary playmates.

Natalie texted Thad, I'm sorry for offering parenting advice. I need to stick to what I know best. Party planning.

Funny, this staycation renewed the very thing she knew all along—Natalie was at her best when she was planning an event for others. The stressors were variables that she'd unnecessarily focused on this past year. But the joy of working to the final goal? That was why she loved her job.

"It is all about the process." She smiled and nearly bowed at the snow people through the glass door.

Lex ran up and barked. "Yes, I know. That was first said about fishing." She let her inside.

But now was the time to dive into the process of finalizing this festival. The only stressors for Natalie were the what-ifs.

Her phone chimed. Thanks. I'm sorry for getting upset. I just need to keep communicating with Brody. We'll figure it out.

And she made a mental note that the "we" he mentioned had nothing to do with her. While Natalie enjoyed time with the MacDougall men, now was the time for the festival. Relationships were too messy for a staycation.

She may as well be working.

And that's exactly what she decided to do.

After lunch on Friday, Thad left the center's kitchen and started down the hall to his office when many voices arose from the living area. He went to see what was going on.

A large rectangular table was set up to one side of the living area, and several women sat around it, various materials scattered about in front of them.

Fran caught his eye and waved from the far end of the table. "Thad, we are your worker elves." Several of the other ladies looked his way and greeted with bubbling energy.

"What's all this?" he asked Susie, who sat closest to where he stood.

"Oh, just some prep for the festival." She had a stack of place cards and a list. "There are some details we hadn't considered for the festival. Natalie reminded Fran, and Fran suggested we have a workday." Susie lowered her voice. "Her sister would be so proud."

"Huh, seems like this should have been something we discussed in one of our meetings." Thad swallowed hard. "I guess I should have looked at the binder more closely."

"No worries, dear. We usually do this closer to the day of. But Natalie made a good point to bump up the preparations today so we could get a sneak peek at how the pageant is coming along." Susie glanced at the door. "Oh, speaking of Natalie, here she comes."

Natalie strode toward them with several bags in each hand. Her gaze skimmed his and she gave a quick smile, then turned her attention to the rest of the group. "Okay, my worker elves. I have all sorts of additional crafts for the Kiddie Korner."

"Kiddie Korner?" Thad blurted.

Natalie stared at him and said matter-of-factly, "It's a craft area for children attending the festival. Tina dresses as Mrs. Klaus and entertains the children while parents peruse the silent auction." She set the bags at the center of the table, then walked past him quickly. "It's all in the binder, Thad," she called out, a singsong reminder that he should know better.

He bobbed his head in acknowledgment. Natalie pulled off her hat, her curls a tad wild, shook off her coat and disappeared to the cloakroom. He followed her, ignoring the stares of the women behind him.

"You really don't have to do all this, Natalie. I'll give myself a crash course on the binder from here on out." He crossed his arms and leaned on the doorjamb. "You should take it easy."

Natalie spun around after hanging her coat. "Take it easy? We are less than two weeks away from the festival." Her smile bedazzled. Almost a little too much. "And besides, we're amping up what we've done in years past. Remember? The binder won't be enough at this point. Taking it easy is not in my vocabulary." She brushed her hands together as if she'd just completed her task. "Excellence only."

He pushed himself off the doorjamb, slightly blocking the entrance. "You know what I mean. You're on a break, remember?"

Her blue eyes searched his. "I'm fine, Thad. Actually, I am more than fine. This is what I love to do. Pretend I never said anything about, well, you know." She brushed past him. "Oh, Carrie is arriving any minute. She told me to be sure there is space for all the parents. She encouraged them to come and give the kids a practice audience."

"For the pageant?"

"Of course."

"Yep, they will be in the chapel. Plenty of seating." Thad scratched his head, conflicted between his heart and his good reason. Natalie was moving at a pace he hadn't seen from her these past couple of weeks—except maybe when she challenged him to put his phone away and start focusing on the festival. Her energy was high, and her demeanor exploded with purpose.

Thad headed to his office to flip through the binder. Seemed their tense moment had no lingering side effects. He had worried about it over the past couple of days without Natalie around the center. Sure, she'd apologized, but the way they had left things was unsettling for Thad. Face-to-face conflict resolution was preferred, but obviously not needed for Natalie. No, this local star was shining her way into full-on festival mode, and while Thad wasn't the kind of guy to be starstruck, he had to resist from wishing there was mistletoe about two minutes ago when all the beauty in the Rapid Falls was facing him in pure determination. The new year couldn't get here fast enough, because keeping things purely platonic with Natalie might prove as rare as a Christmas miracle.

After a quick rundown of the Klaus Kiddie Korner outlined in the binder, Thad left to pick up Brody from school. When they returned, Carrie had set some bins on the small stage in the chapel.

"First to arrive." She held a clipboard and looked for Brody's name. "Ah, you are my donkey. Your costume is right over there." She pointed to a portable rack. "The ears are in the blue bin."

Thad helped Brody with the long brown smock. A tail was attached, and some faux fur was glued along the collar. "Looking good."

"Guess Natalie didn't have her ears?" Brody gazed up at Thad as if on the verge of disappointment.

"Maybe the ears in the bin *are* Natalie's?" Thad's suggestion seemed to satisfy Brody, who dashed over to the bins by the stage. A few more kids had arrived, and some parents were filling in the first few rows of chairs. Natalie was in the lobby, pacing on the phone. All her excitement from earlier had disappeared. She shoved the phone in her pocket. Thad passed by a few parents hurrying their kids into the chapel.

"Natalie, is everything okay?"

She turned to him with a hand on her chest. "It's fine. But we need to come up with an alternative for the centerpieces. The greenery is sold out. Sally's going to have to start from scratch—" Susie carried an arch of flocked garland, and two men followed her with pillars. "Oh, Susie, put that over by the Christmas tree. We'll set that up next week. And I have a fantastic idea for a photo backdrop. It's going to be my little contribution to the festival this year." She folded her hands together and returned her attention to Thad. "There are a million little things to do. I texted Lindsey to go to our storage unit and see what we might have for the centerpiece dilemma."

"You know, fishermen wouldn't pay much attention to the centerpieces if they'd just spent a day on the ice." He winked, trying to lighten the tension.

She rolled her eyes. "Ha ha. We've got it under control, Thad. Mark that idea down for next year."

"Okay, as long as you are feeling good about all this—" He motioned toward the ladies chattering and working away.

"This is a planner's dream." She crossed her arms and rocked back on her heels. "So, do you need something?"

"Uh, no, I was just checking—" He didn't want to bring up his concern for her health again. She'd asked him to not discuss it, and he would respect that. Especially after their argument on Wednesday. "Sounds like you've figured out a solution."

He returned to the chapel. While the pianist was practicing "O Little Town of Bethlehem," Carrie stopped Thad mid-aisle. "Would Brody want to fill in for the narrator? She won't be able to make the rehearsal tonight." She was fiddling with her phone in one hand and gripping her clipboard in the other. "I am wondering if we just move the cast around a bit. It's getting late in the game to not have a narrator at practice."

Thad glanced at Brody who was frantically shaking his head and mouthing "no." "Uh, he's not going to be able to do that."

Carrie scrunched her nose. "The other animals are too young to be the narrator, and the other roles have memorized their lines."

Natalie's voice carried from the lobby. There was an edge in her tone. Thad was worried about her. She needed to step away if this would be too much.

Carrie talked to the group of parents sitting in the first few rows. "Does anyone want to read the narrator role for me?"

Thad rushed forward. "Hey, Carrie. I think Natalie would be willing to volunteer." She needed a break from the chaos of Santa's workshop that exploded all over the living area. And while she probably wouldn't listen to Thad, she'd surely do it for the pageant director.

Carrie rushed past him. "I'll get her." She then called out, "We'll start in five. Everyone, places!"

Chapter Seventeen

Natalie followed Carrie into the chapel. "Uh, there are a lot of parents here." She swallowed, noting that Thad sat in the last row.

"It's good for the kids to have an audience."

Natalie agreed to narrate far too quickly. She hadn't thought this through. When was the last time she had to get up and not only speak in front of a group of people, but read? Maybe in her college rhetoric class, eons ago? And back then, she'd pretty much memorized what she was reading to make sure she didn't confuse words in front of the class.

Sure, this was a kids' production. The script would be simple, right? But even then, reading in front of people made Natalie's stomach hurt.

She weakly smiled at Thad, who grinned as she passed his aisle. Her heart was already racing from the frustration out in the winter wonder mess of festival prep. Now it leaped all sorts of different ways as she passed not one, or two but three rows filled with parents.

Carrie handed Natalie the script as she took her place behind a podium on stage left. Brody waved from his flock of animals, and the three wise men took center stage.

"Okay, start here—" Carrie pointed to the top line.

And Natalie began to read the Christmas story.

She stumbled on a few words, but easily recovered, until she looked up, and a man in the front row stared at her... mouth? Did she say something wrong? Uncertainty welled at the back of her throat. She tried to remain calm. Susie passed by the door of the chapel and did a double take when she caught Natalie's eye.

Yep, they have me reading in front of all these practical strangers.

Natalie glanced over at Thad. He offered a reassuring smile, the one that had promised comfort and acceptance in the not-so-distant past. For a moment, she may as well have been wrapped in his hug, breathing in his cedar and spice scent and enjoying his company inside a lantern-lit igloo. During this speaking debut on stage, Thad MacDougall was her happy place.

Her gaze fell away from his and she bit her lip, staring hard at the script. What happened to her perseverance?

"Uh, Natalie?" Carrie whispered from her front-row spot and nodded to the podium.

"Oops," Natalie said and found her spot on the page. She continued to read, but now, distraction got the best of her. Suddenly, she couldn't get the words out right, and her throat tightened.

Her palms began to sweat. Moisture appeared where her finger had been trailing under the printed words. She managed to finish her next part. People shifted in the front row and a couple of women whispered to each other.

She shouldn't be here. This was not what she signed up for. In fact, she hadn't signed up for anything at all. All the stress from earlier seemed to sit on her chest like the whole sheep herd that was making its way to the front of the stage.

She was dizzy.

Once again, she looked over at Thad. His smile was gone, and he began to stand.

"Um, I don't feel so good." She interrupted the baa-ing of the sheep and hurried down the stage steps.

Susie and Thad flanked her as she took a seat in the back row.

Susie put a hand on her shaking knee. "You are as pale as snow, Nattie."

"I can't breathe." She bent over and put her head between her legs.

Thad's firm hand pressed on her back. "Natalie, what can I do?"

"Uh, you can take over narrating, for one," she said in the direction of the floor.

"I am surprised you volunteered for this." Susie put words to her astonished second take from earlier. "You've never loved public speaking."

Natalie lifted up slowly. "That's an understatement."

"You mean this is because you had to read from the script?" Thad gripped his chin and searched Natalie's lips—for an answer, she was certain.

"Um, I was a donkey for a reason, Thad." Natalie quietly laughed and wiped her sweaty forehead with the back of her hand. "I think I need to go home."

"Yes, I'll drive you." Susie helped her stand. "I don't want you driving home after a panic attack."

Natalie blinked away tears as embarrassment heated her neck. "I can't believe I got stage fright here, in front of a bunch of children."

Susie gathered her in a hug. "You were doing great, Nattie. Don't be hard on yourself."

"Let me know if you need anything, Natalie." Thad squeezed her arm and headed to the podium. "I'm a phone call away."

"Thank you." Natalie's voice was weak. She leaned into Susie, thankful she was out of the spotlight. Natalie was a behind-the-scenes kind of person, she'd known that all along. The spotlight had lost its luster far quicker than her blood pressure could keep up.

When they pulled up to Natalie's house, a familiar car was parked in the driveway. Lindsey waved from the driver's seat. Natalie hopped out and ran around the car to greet her best friend.

"Surprise," Lindsey exclaimed and wrapped her arms around Natalie. Her long black hair smelled like lavender and mint, and her fuzzy wool hat was soft against Natalie's cheek.

"What are you doing here?" Natalie pulled back, still feeling a little woozy.

"I thought I would help with the festival." She gestured to her back seat filled with boxes from the storage unit. "I know you said you would meet me halfway to grab the stuff. But—" Lindsey tilted her head in concern. "You look pale."

"It's cold, let's go inside and talk. Just a sec." Natalie returned to Susie's car.

Susie rolled her window down. "Everything okay? That's Lindsey, right? I met her at the CF Gala."

"Yes, she surprised me with a visit. Do you want to come in for some hot chocolate?"

"No, I'll get back and see that everything's going as planned." She gave a thumbs-up. "Enjoy spending time with your friend."

After saying goodbye, Lindsey and Natalie hurried inside. Lex was just as excited to see Lindsey—the woman who treated Lex like her own baby. After hanging up her winter gear, she immediately plopped down on the couch and invited Lex to snuggle.

"Good thing Mom isn't here to see this. She adores Lex but not fur on the cushions."

"Oh, that's just being part of the family, isn't it Lex?" Lindsey proceeded to tilt her cheek in position for Lex's kisses.

Natalie giggled as she fixed two cups of cocoa. She placed the mugs on the coffee table, flipped the switch for the gas fireplace and sat down on the other side of Lex, tucking her legs beneath her. "So, find anything that will work for our centerpieces?"

"Yes, I did," she said in her playful voice, rubbing Lex behind the ears. Glancing over at Natalie, she conceded to Lex, "Okay, I am going to talk to Miss Staycation Faker now." Her lip quirked wryly, and her dark brown eyes glimmered in disapproval. "How are you in charge of this festival?"

Natalie guffawed. "I am not."

"Sounds to me that you are."

"Well, I wasn't. But then we got some really great donors and more table reservations. People are counting on this festival. I just wanted to be sure it was successful."

"Has it not been successful in the past?"

"Well, yes. But after all I've learned this past year, we can amp it up to really knock socks off. Especially since we need to raise funds."

"Okay, Nat. But I didn't like seeing you looking so worn out when you pulled up in the driveway." Lindsey reached for her cocoa. "Exactly what I suspected last time we spoke. And exactly why I am here. Kick up your feet, Natalie. I am taking over."

Natalie tossed her head back in a laugh. "You are no planner, Linds."

"And you need to take care of yourself."

"You sound like Thad," she mumbled and drank from her mug.

"Oh, really? So *Thaddeus* is a wise guy. And *he's* the director. Shouldn't you just let him take over?"

"If he took over, they'd have a rugged ice fishing tournament to kick off what is supposed to be an elegant Christmas extravaganza."

"Ice fishing?"

"Yes, he suggested it when we were thinking about how to raise more money. Silly, right?"

Lindsey shrugged. They both slurped their drinks. "What happened today? Why did you get dropped off?"

"I had a panic attack—" She raised a hand to signal for Lindsey to not jump to any conclusions. "Not because of overdoing it with planning—but because of public speaking."

"What? Why would you get up and speak in front of people?"

"I know! But I was so caught up in making the festival perfect, I jumped into it without thinking."

"Because you were overdoing it." Lindsey reiterated what Natalie denied doing.

Natalie set her mug down and sighed, pushing back into the couch cushions. "The only thing I was overdoing was ignoring my boundaries. Honestly, Lindsey, working on the festival, with some of my favorite people, in one of my homes away from home like the center…it's hardly been stressful."

"Really?"

"I guess the most stressful part was when we found out that out-of-towners were contributing. I wanted to prove that the festival was worth the trip. For Rapid Falls."

"I know how much Rapid Falls means to you. But you

don't have to prove yourself, Natalie. How many times do I have to tell you that?"

Natalie shrank back into the cushions even more. Lindsey was making this about Natalie, but wasn't it about the retirement community and her town? "Lindsey, I know I get carried away, but the only reason I had that episode today was because I had to get up in front of people."

"Because you were caught up in planning when you should have been relaxing."

"You're right." Natalie wasn't supposed to be doing anything right now. She thought about this afternoon. At first glance, the workshop atmosphere was picture-perfect to her planner heart. And later, a desperate glance at Thad had been the perfect source of comfort she needed on the stage. If blood pressure depended on moral support, then she'd throw out her meds this very minute. As long as Thad was nearby. Her heart somersaulted at such a thought. She shouldn't think that way. Any other familiar face in the room would have comforted her.

She watched the flames flicker behind the glass. "I wish that we could be guaranteed extra revenue."

"You said you have donors to impress. Did you promise them anything extra from last year?"

"No, everything listed on the save-the-date is the same."

"Maybe Thad was on to something."

"What do you mean?"

"A fishing tournament. What better way to kick off a festive weekend in an Iowa December?"

"I didn't really consider it at all. Didn't seem to fit with the festival. But Thad is pretty in-tune to what others need, so maybe." These past couple of weeks, Thad had opened up to her beyond festival details. And when she trusted him with her health issue, he didn't look at her as less valuable. He seemed to support her need to take it easy by constantly checking with her. He cared so much for his son, the retirement folks, and he seemed to care for her, too.

All this time, Natalie had inserted herself as the resident event planner. But maybe this staycation wasn't just for her health, but her heart?

After the pageant rehearsal, Thad and Brody helped sort the craft materials for the Kiddie Korner. But mostly, Thad waited for Susie to return. He pulled out his phone to text Natalie, then shoved it back in his pocket. Disturbing her was the last thing he wanted to do after being the one who suggested she speak in the first place.

Helping Natalie stay healthy had only sent her into a panic attack. Seemed that Thad's intention, no matter how good, led to disaster. Why did he feel the need to be her hero incognito? Turned out, he was more like a busybody who didn't know the full picture.

Susie walked in with a to-go order from Sweet Lula's for Fran and her friends. No wonder it took her so long to return. She'd made a pit stop. Thad quickly finished up what he was doing.

"Hey, Thad and Brody, I am glad you're still here." Susie walked over and handed them each a cup. "Drinking chocolate. Marge suggested you two would enjoy it."

"Thank you." Thad gave Brody his cup, took his own then motioned for Susie to sit with him on the couch. "How is Natalie?"

"She'll be fine. A friend is with her now." Susie reached over and shimmied the last cup from the to-go carrier on the coffee table.

"I didn't realize public speaking was an issue for her."

"It always has been. But really, it's public reading that gives her the most fits." She pushed her glasses up and then sipped her drink.

"Ah, that makes sense with dyslexia." Thad glanced over at Brody, who'd refused the narrator part. "I feel bad because I had suggested she fill in for the narrator."

"Oh, you couldn't have known." She dipped her chin, looking over her glasses at him. "Why did you suggest her, though?"

Thad hesitated to speak. Natalie didn't want anyone to know about her blood pressure. "She cared about the pageant. Seemed a good fit."

"You two have spent a lot of time together." She smiled behind the cup at her lips. "She's a very easy person to be with, isn't she?"

"I'm thankful that she's persisted for the festival's sake." Thad avoided discussing how much he enjoyed being with Natalie. "She's never once complained about having to help. I appreciate her for that. And she has a way of empathizing on a deeper level." Her willingness to help was unlike anything he received during his rocky years of marriage.

"Natalie went through a lot of growing pains. I tutored her for five years. She's come such a long way." Susie offered a genuine, non-matchmaking smile. "But we are so glad she still makes Rapid Falls her home."

"She's given me an appreciation for this place. The traditions are astounding." He looked over at Brody again. "I guess I should thank her because she's not only been there for me, but Brody, too—" He scoffed inwardly. "She really seems to care about him." *And me.*

Oh, man, Thad should not be thinking this way, especially here, with all these people indiscreetly pushing the new director toward their golden child.

Susie just sat and looked at him intently. "And what are you going to do about it?"

"About what?"

"About that angsty look in your eye that tells me that this isn't all about Natalie caring for your son."

"Are you a knitting club member?" Thad gave her a wry smile, and laughed, running his hand through his hair. "Even if it was about something more, there is nothing to be done about it."

"Why not?"

"Because this is a place I want to be for a long time. I don't have the greatest track record with relationships. If I mess anything up, it wouldn't just be between Natalie and me." He glanced around the room at all the familiar faces—Fran, Tina, Edward Shaw, a few ladies from the assisted living wing. "Everyone would be affected."

Thad had finally seen the fruits of this move to Rapid Falls with Brody's affirmation the other day under the Christmas tree. First, admitting his affection for Natalie right now would no doubt end up whispered in her ear within a matter of cribbage games. He wasn't sure if he was worried more about her rejection, or what might happen if he failed to meet her expectations as a significant other.

How could he continue to grow roots in Rapid Falls if he ever broke the heart of their favorite event planner?

Chapter Eighteen

Early Monday morning, Natalie woke up with a stuffy nose and a low-grade fever. She curled up under a throw blanket with a box of tissues, praying and planning in her mind.

Besides taking Gigi to Saint George's on Sunday, Lindsey and Natalie had spent most of the weekend working on the photo backdrop for the festival. The large six-foot-by-eight-foot plywood was covered in sparkly white felt with beaded snowflakes sewn around the border. But that wasn't all Natalie thought about. An ice fishing tournament was rolling around in her fuzzy head.

When Lindsey woke up, she flipped on the fireplace and joined her on the couch. "The sun's not even up yet. Why are we?"

"I couldn't sleep. I wonder if it's feasible to try and put together a fishing tournament—" She sneezed and blew her nose. "We have less than two weeks to get the word out."

"Oh, Natalie, you sound miserable."

"Tell me about it." She coughed into her sleeve. "We should have worked on the backdrop in the house, not the garage."

Lindsey tsked. "Not sure it was that. I think you overdid it on this supposed staycation." She stretched her arms and yawned. "I feel great."

"Rub it in, why don't you?"

Lex jumped in the middle of the couch between their feet. They laughed, then discussed the plan forming in Natalie's mind. Every time Lindsey mentioned *Thaddeus*, Natalie couldn't help but giggle—whether coughing or sneezing. It was a very exhilarating yet physically uncomfortable conversation.

When the sun rose, they moved their lounge session to the kitchen. Natalie's coughing fits were just getting worse.

"You really overdid it, Natalie."

"How many times are you going to remind me?" Natalie sounded like she was underwater. She opened the cooling teakettle and stuck her face in the residual steam, trying to breathe through her nostrils as best as she could. "I don't have time for this."

"Why don't you let him take the reins?" Lindsey stirred some peppermint chips into her cocoa. "It was his idea."

Natalie dunked her tea bag up and down as she shuffled across the wood floor in her fuzzy socks. The morning sunlight was bright, yet not offering any warmth in these single digits. She sat across from Lindsey at the table. "Thad had mentioned feeling defeated by nothing working out the way he planned." She cinched her flannel robe closer around her matching pajamas to ward off the chill. "I want to surprise him. With a good *unplanned* plan. Sound silly? I really can't think straight right now."

Lindsey smiled wide. "Sounds like you are smitten with *Thaddeus*."

The bergamot tea with honey looked like tea but Natalie couldn't smell a thing, although she feigned sniffing the stuff to pause her visible reaction at Lindsey's teasing. Yet, she was tingly on the inside. "It doesn't really matter at this point. I just want to surprise him, okay?"

Lindsey raised her hands in surrender. "Okay, you're

getting snippety with that cold. Give me the address of the parks and rec office. I'll drop by. They close at noon?"

"That's what the website says. But I should just go with you. They know me—"

Lindsey stood and walked away saying, "There is no way anyone will want you to come to their office today. I'm going to go take an extra dose of vitamin C right now and get ready."

"Thank you, Linds," Natalie called out, unable to keep her smile from growing, no matter how crummy she felt.

"Excuse me?"

Thad looked up from the grant application on his computer screen. A tall woman with straight black hair and olive skin stood with a knit hat in her manicured hands. "Hi *Thadeu*— I mean, you must be Thad, right?"

"Yes, I'm Thad, and you are?"

She crossed his office with an outstretched hand, and they shook. "I am Natalie's business partner, Lindsey. Natalie asked me to drop by some new centerpieces. She told me to tell you that they aren't as pretty as Sally's, but they'll have to do since you have more tables reserved." Lindsey averted her gaze as if she were taking inventory of the ceiling tiles. "Oh, and she wanted me to suggest that some of the original centerpieces can be set on the buffet table and around the living area for added decor."

"Sounds good." Why hadn't she come herself? Thad grimaced, worried that Natalie had found out about his conversation with Susie. He half expected the message relay, seeing as how he'd practically admitted his feelings for the woman. Usually, Natalie stopped by on Sunday. But he hadn't seen her yesterday. And he had looked. Especially since that was Brody's first session with Susie. Thad kind of hoped Natalie would show up and see for herself. "Um, why didn't she just come tell me?"

"Oh, I should have mentioned—" Lindsey widened her eyes and shook her head. "She is sick, sick, sick. Doesn't need to be around people right now. But she suggested that Brody come over and finish the snow people." She leaned a palm on the desk and spoke from the corner of her mouth. "Believe me, it's a little depressing to see the headless guy day in and day out."

Thad chuckled. "Will do. Brody is at his mom's tonight, but maybe on Wednesday—"

"No!" The abrupt word seemed to surprise her as much as it had him. "I mean, please come today. It would really cheer up the patient. You can finish the snow people."

"Uh, or you can—"

Lindsey's shoulders drooped, and she flung her head back and groaned. Strangely similar to his nine-year-old son. This woman was…interesting. "I really shouldn't spell it out for you. But… Natalie wants to see you, Thad."

"Really?"

"Just come to the backyard on your way home—at five o'clock to be exact." Lindsey spun around and disappeared down the hall, leaving Thad a little confused, and a lot curious. Why did Natalie want to see him, and was this really about snow people?

He looked at the clock. Three hours until he'd find some answers. He sat back in his office chair and positioned his hands behind his head, unable to contain a large grin.

Natalie wanted to see him, and after two days apart, Thad could hardly wait to see her, too.

The Christmas lights on Natalie's house were bright reminders of all the time he'd spent with her. And his heart flipped because of it. Not because he expected this requested visit was about matters of the heart, but because the twinkles and candy canes marked one of the many

Christmas memories he made with his son and the beautiful event planner. Even if she'd soon speed off to events large and small, at least he had a chance to see her tonight. In the most curious way.

He pulled into the driveway and took out the cedar wreath with ribbon and tapered candles. If Thad caved to the vulnerability of romance at all—a notion he'd avoided after it led him astray once before—then he would have to admit the moment he might have first fallen for Natalie Cooper—in the boutique behind the counter, to be exact. Natalie's admiration of this piece struck him with the dilemma of second-guessing what was best for him. Playing life safe or being with Natalie?

He tromped through the snow around the side of the house to the back gate, holding on to the centerpiece. The gate was open and fresh boot prints disappeared around the house. As he followed the prints, a sensor triggered a floodlight, lighting up the snow people. But all three were finished. And they had hats and eyes and noses and…fishing poles?

A knocking rapped behind him. Natalie waved through the glass, fully dressed in her snow gear, with a hat, a scarf and a rosy-colored nose. She opened the door. "Hey, Thad," she said in a raspy voice. He started toward her, but she shook her head waving a manila envelope around. "I'm sick. Don't come too close."

"Natalie, I hope it wasn't from—" He looked over his shoulder at the snow people. "Playing in the snow?"

Natalie laughed. "No. Lindsey did the honors. But we aren't playing. Thad, I wanted to surprise you." She crossed her arms over her thick winter coat and stepped outside, closing the door behind her. "I know that sometimes my persistence gets the best of me, and even then, you were checking to make sure I wasn't…" She coughed in her arm, then glanced over her shoulder at Lindsey, who was sitting in the window seat. She waved at them both. Natalie turned back to him. "You made sure I wasn't overdoing it health-wise. There's just something about you, Thad, that makes me feel safe to share everything…even share my health issues." A coy smile grew on her reddened lips. "I know your life turned out differently than you expected—and things didn't go as planned. But I wanted you to be the first to know that your unplanned plan… Well, it's going to happen." She reached out the manila envelope but hesitated when she noticed the centerpiece. "Wait, why do you have that?"

"You have made an impression on me, too, Miss Cooper." He traded her the centerpiece for the envelope. "I'll never forget the way you admired Sally's artistic piece. And quoted Steve Jobs." They both laughed. While her gaze lingered on the pretty arrangement, Thad's gaze lingered on her.

Could he move past this season denying his feelings for this woman? Was he denying them or shoving them aside because he didn't want to risk more heartache? What if there was no heartache with Natalie, though?

"Your turn," Natalie blurted like they were participating in a gift exchange.

Thad opened the manila envelope and pulled out a flyer:

The Annual RFRC Christmas Festival Kickoff
Ice Fish-A-Thon
Entry fee will give you a timed session
on the lake and a raffle ticket for prizes
at the evening Christmas festival.
Sign up by December 22

"Are you serious?" A rush of excitement filled every corner of his chest. "I thought you didn't think it would work."

"And you thought that I should read a script in front of all those people." Natalie smirked playfully.

Thad rubbed his jaw. "So, you talked with Susie."

"It's okay. Really. I am glad I left when I did or else I might have gotten a lot of people sick."

Thad looked down at the flyer once more. "So, what did you call this? My unplanned plan?"

Natalie smiled. "Yep, you have some great ideas, even if the event planner wasn't on board at first. Thanks for this." She nodded down at the centerpiece.

"You're welcome. It's a good reminder for you." Thad resisted closing in the gap. Last time this centerpiece was between them, he could see the amber threads in her eyes, smell the floral scent of her shampoo.

"A reminder?"

"That you're beautiful." He'd said it then, and he meant it now, more than ever. She blushed, but a coughing fit brought Thad to his senses. "You need to go inside. The temp is dropping by the second."

She nodded as she continued to cough in her upper arm since the centerpiece was in her hands. "Thank you so much, Thad. Pray I get better for the festival." He nodded and she hurried into the house.

Thad spun around, wanting to jump in childish glee. He hadn't been this happy in a long time. And it had little to do with fishing.

The snow people with fishing poles made more sense now. But nothing else really made sense at all. Just a couple of weeks ago, Thad's plan for a fresh start in Rapid Falls to be close to Brody seemed to be enough. After all the expectations Thad had failed to meet in his marriage, and during his time away from Brody, Natalie showed up and offered something he'd forgotten about.

Falling in love wasn't reasonable at all.

And Thad was okay with that.

Chapter Nineteen

On the morning of the Ice Fish-A-Thon, Thad and Brody set up their fishing spot as dawn went from indigo to gray to a vibrant pink. The air was crisp without the slightest breeze. A perfect start.

If the numbers were correct, this tournament would bring in a significant amount of funding for the retirement community. Thad had anticipated this weekend more than he ever thought he would. Not only had he followed in the petite footsteps of a beautiful event planner and poured some heart and soul into planning this ice fishing tournament, but he'd connected with other fishermen in Rapid Falls and felt all the more part of the community.

Thad and Brody fished in the first round. Seven other fishermen dotted about the small lake. The owners of the orchard sat at their hole to their left and had been the most generous with their financial pledge to the tournament. Not surprising after Lance Hudson and Thad had discussed fishing gear and good spots around the area for over an hour when Lance had visited his grandmother at the retirement community. His enthusiasm for fishing was obvious. Now, Lance's wife, Piper, and their daughter, Maelyn, huddled around the hole with warm drinks in their hands, while Lance finished setting up. Truly a family affair.

Brody rummaged through his tackle box beside Thad,

seemingly just as excited as his dad for this day. The boy's countenance had become lighter since he'd started his tutoring sessions. Homework was still not his favorite thing, but if he struggled with it, he was content knowing Susie could help him. Everything had clicked into place for Thad to live up to the father he had expected to be from Brody's first breath. Father and son, side by side on the ice—the only place he wanted to be in this moment.

Would they ever experience a family affair around the MacDougall fishing spot like the Hudsons had? After all the encouraging words from Natalie, Thad could finally hope for family again, without cringing at the weightiness of what it implied.

"There's Lex!" Brody pointed across the lake. Natalie was waving from the far bank, where she stood with Lex. "Why didn't they come on this side?"

Thad chuckled and reminded Brody what happened last time. His phone began to vibrate in his coat pocket.

"We can't keep meeting like this," Natalie teased when he answered. This was the third time this week that they were in the same place at the same time but couldn't really talk because of the busy preparations of the festival.

"What do you think?" Thad waved his arm at all the fishermen. "The tourney is underway, and we've got three more rounds before noon."

Lex barked. "Well, Lex is very pleased." She laughed. "Truly, Thad, it's amazing. But I'd better go. Lindsey gave me permission to help with setup at the center. Isn't that sweet of her?" The ongoing joke since Natalie recovered from her cold had been Lindsey's strict watch over Natalie's dealings with the festival. Thad was glad her friend helped Natalie manage her effort for the sake of her health.

Although Lindsey seemed to be around even when Natalie was in proximity enough for Thad to have a face-to-face

200 The Unplanned Christmas Family

conversation and to gauge if what he had been feeling was reciprocated by Natalie. After the night in her backyard, Thad had made up his mind. Natalie was the only woman he could see in his future—the one person he'd invite to his fishing hole with Brody, any day.

"Hey, Thad?"

"Yep?"

"I'm really proud of you." Her voice was soft, genuine. When was the last time someone had told him that? "This is going to be a huge success if our registration is correct."

"Well, a beautiful event planner taught me a thing or two about tenacity. No man in Rapid Falls could say no when I recruited them." He squinted in her direction. "I wish I could see you."

She didn't say anything at first. Had he said something wrong? Maybe he was being too forward. A sigh came through the phone. "Me, too" was all she said, and it was enough.

A month ago, Natalie had an encounter with the parking lot attendant at her grandmother's retirement center and senior living residence. Now, the guy had become one of her favorite people in Rapid Falls, and she hoped that he felt the same as she did. Because with the busy spring just ahead, Natalie was preparing to carve out more time at home between gigs. Her pesky blood pressure had taught her a thing or two about balance these past few weeks, with the help of her best friend and that handsome director who cared enough to remind her to slow down every once in a while. And she didn't quite mind taking things slow and easy if *Thaddeus* was around.

She entered the center before the festival started, delighted by the transformation of the spaces. Thankfully, Lindsey allowed her to assist in the decoration day—it was her absolute favorite part of an event, and her best friend couldn't deny her the pleasure of helping. The lobby glittered with twinkle lights along the ceiling and around the doorways. An ornate decorative sleigh sat in one corner, ready for gift donations to the women's shelter, and in the other corner stood the photo backdrop, sparkly and wintry in every way.

Natalie hung up her coat and scarf and smoothed down her black A-line dress, which also donned a few sparkles— around the cuffs, collar and knee-length hem. She spun around, noting the swoosh against her legs, feeling pretty— no, beautiful, like Thad had said twice now.

On that thought, she practically floated past the dining room that glowed with the hurricane vase centerpieces beneath garland strung from the ceiling. Darcie's distant voice and clinking dishes carried from the kitchen door.

Natalie hadn't seen the silent auction set up around the living space and was amazed at the sight. Marge and Lula had arranged the items on tables along the perimeter of the space. They used dark green velveteen tablecloths, and strategically placed Sally's original centerpieces between the different sections of items. Natalie walked over to the fireplace, running her hands along the mantel, which no longer held old decorations but an evergreen arrangement, similar to Sally's centerpieces, stretching along the surface.

"Elegant, huh?" Thad's rich voice spun her around. "Wow, Natalie, you are—" He pulled his hands from the pockets of his perfectly pressed suit pants and straightened his black sports coat. "Beautiful."

Third time's a charm? Natalie smiled, noting that his red tie was the same shade as the lipstick she'd bought today. "Thank you, Thad. You look very handsome."

After being sick for a couple days, and then joining the

bustle of festival preparations sporadically, being in this space with Thad, alone, was surreal. Dreamlike. Dreamy.

He walked up to her, his chocolate gaze ever warm. "Are we ready for this?" His lopsided smile was adorable.

"Look where the process got us." Natalie winked and glanced around. When she locked gazes with him again, Thad gathered her hands in his, sending electricity through her, enough to outshine the thousands of glowing lights.

"Natalie, your unplanned plan has been one of the greatest gifts of my life. Today was nearly perfect."

"Nearly?"

His fingers laced with hers and he pulled their hands to rest on his chest. "After spending so much time together this past month, I would have almost had Lex crash the Ice Fish-a-Thon if it meant spending that time with you."

Natalie's breath hitched on the swoonworthiness of his sweet words. She softly laughed, then shook her head, recalling the day Lex got away. "Could you imagine—" Before she could speak any further, he kissed her. Her eyes fluttered shut, and she leaned into his embrace. If Natalie had known the festival would turn out this way, she would have never been concerned at all.

But then again, the process had been her favorite part. Well, second favorite.

Thad pulled away and brushed his thumb along her cheek. "Think you can squeeze me into your busy life?"

"Think you want a bossy planner around?" Only Thad MacDougall filled her vision, her thoughts, her heart.

"I don't know, Miss Cooper. After the successful morning, you might have to scoot over and make room for this planner extraordinaire." He wagged his eyebrows, and they both laughed.

Natalie caught a glimpse of the mistletoe hanging above them. "Hey, did you kiss me because of that?" she teased.

Thad narrowed his eyes. "If that kiss was only the mistletoe kind, then I haven't done my job." He pressed his lips to hers more firmly this time and cradled her face with both hands. Natalie melted into the man who was quickly initiating a new and most favorite Christmas tradition: the festival kiss—or two.

Epilogue

The Christmas Festival was going to be the perfect pre-party, Natalie considered as she tried on her wedding dress one last time.

Lindsey straightened the train in the back and popped up, ogling at her through the mirror. "This is absolutely gorgeous, Natalie. And one of a kind."

"Of course it is. After all the weddings we planned this year, I can't just pick any old dress." Natalie couldn't believe the last wedding of the year would be hers.

"Is *Thaddeus* all set?"

"Yes. He went ahead and got everything done so he could focus on the fishing tournament."

"He's got priorities, that one." Lindsey chuckled, shaking her head.

Natalie smiled, knowing that if anyone had their priorities straight, it was Thad MacDougall. This past year had been a blur with standout heartfelt moments of his surprise backyard picnics, Sweet Lula to-go runs and his last-minute helping hand at nearby events. Whenever they'd talk during her busy times, he was the voice of calm, encouragement and especially flattery. Oh my, if Thad was perfect in any way, it was by extinguishing all Natalie's insecurities and making her feel appreciated.

Every single moment with Thad was encapsulated in

her heart, and she was so excited for the million more that she knew were ahead.

After they left the city, Natalie grew more anxious to get to Rapid Falls. She'd promised Brody that he could help with Christmas lights again. At least this year, she'd given herself a few more days to get them up before the Tour of Lights.

Rapid Falls was covered in snow as usual. They passed Jim's Grocery, the retirement community, then turned on Birch Street. The Victorian house was as stately as ever. Sean Peters was out hanging up Christmas lights and waved as she drove past.

Lindsey sighed. "Their backyard wedding was one of my favorites. I especially loved their nieces, the cute flower girls."

"Lottie and Ava are very sweet. And last I heard, Elisa is pregnant."

"Glad they have a big house for all those littles." Lindsey chuckled.

When they pulled into the driveway, Lance Hudson's truck was parked on the curb, and Thad and Brody got out.

"Thanks again, Lance." Thad waved and shut the passenger door. Lindsey went into the house to tend to Lex.

"Did his fishing spot live up to the buzz?" Natalie waved as Lance pulled away.

"It was cool," Brody answered, running past them to go inside.

Natalie called to him, "Lights, then hot chocolate, okay?"

"Okay! First Lex, though."

Thad wrapped her in a big hug. "It's getting chilly. How about hot chocolate first?"

"If you want. I mean, it's not the order of events I had envisioned," she jested, tapping her chin as if considering the ramifications. She snuggled closer for warmth.

"Whatever you say, boss." Thad kissed the top of her head. "How was the dress?"

"Perfect, as it has been the past three times I've visited it."

Amusement filled his face and his brown eyes shone beneath the fur trim of his earflap cap. "I can't wait."

"Me, neither. The process has gone on long enough, huh?" She brushed her fingers on his forehead, then propped up on her tiptoes to kiss him again.

"I'd say," he muttered.

"Come on, you two!" Brody called from the porch, holding on to Lex by the leash. "I want to hang up lights before I do my homework." Lex barked her agreement.

Natalie and Thad complied, walking up to Brody and Lex, hand in hand, ready for another Christmas season of wishes come true in Rapid Falls.

* * * * *

If you liked this story from Angie Dicken,
check out her previous Love Inspired books:

Her Chance at Family
His Sweet Surprise
Once Upon a Farmhouse

Available now from Love Inspired!
Find more great reads at www.LoveInspired.com.

Dear Reader,

I hope you enjoyed the third book in the Heartland Sweethearts series. Rapid Falls, Iowa, is filled with amazing people, don't you think? The story world is modeled after my first experiences of living in Iowa. My Texas husband and I were amazed with the true winter wonderland, shocked by the low temps, but dared to venture into the cold like a true Midwesterner. I remember the fun of taking my own sons down Main Street, which was filled with people spreading Christmas cheer. And I'll never forget my husband gathering our small boys to learn to ice fish. I don't think they caught anything, nor did they get interrupted by a friendly golden retriever, but they had a blast. Most of all, my family has collected many special moments focused on the culmination of the season's festivities—the birth of Christ. May you look forward to the beauty of Christmas every year!

Angie Dicken
angiedicken.com